Keepers

RUSSELL H. GREENAN

St. Martin's Press
New York

c. 1

Library of Congress Cataloging in Publication Data

Greenan, Russell H.
    Keepers.

    I. Title.
PZ4.G7982Ke   [PS3557.R376]   813'.5'4   78-19410
ISBN 0-312-45106-7

/3L

MAY 1 4 '79

For Laura and Bill Schlesinger

PART ONE

Although Richard Vaughn's mad brother Nigel is kept guarded on his family's Scarp Island estate, a seemingly accidental drowning soon leads to the conclusion that there is someone else on the island whose madness might not be so easy to confine.

The nurse had brown curly hair with ringlets so precisely formed they might have been of cast bronze or carved teakwood. Her dress, a light cotton frock with short cuffed sleeves, was brown too. She filled it pleasingly.

Osgood knocked the ash from his cigarette in the abalone shell, regarded her frankly and said, "I always thought he was simpleminded, Miss Danziger, but now Uncle Richard tells me he's actually a lunatic."

"Did Mr. Vaughan mention the need for secrecy?" she asked.

"He sure did. I mean, I understand why he doesn't want people to know. It's just that it caught me by surprise. Is it true he's going to run for governor next year?"

To avoid meeting his forthright gaze, the girl swung around in her swivel chair and fell to contemplating what lay outside the half-open casement window—an unkempt patch of sunburnt lawn, a stand of tilted scraggly spruce trees, an outcrop of weatherworn granite shaped like a crude tombstone, a thin gray strip of beach, and, finally, the dark blue sea beneath the light blue sky. "I have no idea," she answered primly. "You'll have to ask him that question yourself."

"I will," Edward Osgood said, a trace of insolence in his voice. "Politics must be a tricky business. I'll bet if people found out he had a brother who was crazy—and dangerous, too—that would louse up his chances. They'd start to wonder how normal Richard Vaughan was himself, wouldn't they? I took a couple of courses in political science at college. Got pretty good grades, too. I guess he explained, I'm not a male nurse or anything like that. The only reason I'm here is because when we were all at a family wedding in Bristol, Uncle Richard happened to tell my mother he was looking for a trustworthy person and, on the spur of the moment, I volunteered. Of course the money isn't sensational but I'll have a chance to get a little sunshine. Except for a week at the Vineyard, I've never lived on an island before. How's the swimming, Miss Danziger?"

The nurse glanced at him from the corners of her hazel eyes, then resumed her survey of the vista. "Very nice," she said reservedly. "Were you told much about Nigel's illness? Did Mr. Vaughan give you a detailed description?"

The youth drew on his cigarette, and, letting the smoke drift from his moving mouth, answered, "Yes, he went over everything. Warned me to watch myself and to stay out of Nigel's reach, because he can be pretty violent at times. But I can deal with the physical end of it. I used to lift weights at the Providence Y, and do a little boxing."

"All the same, you mustn't take any chances. Nigel is strong . . . and crafty. He's capable of some wild behavior."

Outside the window a herring gull swooped into view. For several seconds it hung motionless in the clear morning air, a splash of dingy white on the azure sky, then it dipped gracefully behind the dark spruce trees and was gone.

"Such as?" Osgood inquired.

"Well, your predecessor, Mr. MacKenzie—Nigel

broke his arm. That's why he resigned and went back to Scotland."

"I heard about it. Didn't the guy make a big fuss?"

"No. Mr. Vaughan paid him a rather large severance bonus, I understand," she replied, turning her head an inch or two to give him another look. "Nigel never really took to Mr. MacKenzie. One day he became annoyed about some trivial matter, pulled the poor man's arm through the bars, and snapped it at the elbow. There have been a few other incidents, too. He hurled a pot of boiling water at the nurse who was here before me, though luckily most of it missed her. I guess you were told that Nigel had been institutionalized prior to his being sent to Scarp. It was at one of those asylums—a place in Montana—that he committed a murder."

"A murder? Honest to God?"

"Yes, but that was some time ago. He strangled another inmate with a pair of suspenders. Shortly after that he was transferred back East. Mr. Vaughan said the attendants out there began to mistreat him because of what he had done, so he arranged to have him brought to Rhode Island. For a while Nigel was kept at a local sanitarium, Parkstone, and then they shipped him out here."

Osgood's handsome face grew pensive. "Uncle Richard never mentioned a murder," he said. "That's spooky. In fact, the whole situation is kind of weird—isn't it, Miss Danziger? I suppose he could transfer him because he's got political clout. Must be illegal, though. I mean, you just can't lock a person up in your own private prison, even if he is a relative and nutty as a Baby Ruth."

"Nigel's been certified mad, and Mr. Vaughan is a lawyer." She swung around again to confront him. "I'm sure he's not breaking any laws. Years ago, people often looked after the disturbed members of their families at home, if they were able to. The senile or demented were kept in attic rooms. It was common practice, and is probably still being done in rural areas."

5

"But this man has bars on his windows and doors."

"Yes, for his own good. They allow him some contact with the outside world. Otherwise he'd be shut up completely." The girl took a ball-point pen from her desk and clicked it abstractedly. In the quiet office it sounded like the cocking of a pistol. "Your uncle's feelings for his brother are quite strong. He brought him here so that he could care for him better, so that he could provide him with the personal attention he'd never get elsewhere. You mustn't think of the patient as a prisoner."

Osgood smiled skeptically. "That's what he is though, isn't he? But since he's homicidal, I guess it's okay. Aren't you a little nervous, working around a fellow like that? You're only a woman."

"Nervous? No. However, I don't take any risks. For the most part, Nigel and I get along extremely well. I'm sure he likes me."

"That's not hard to understand," said the youth boldly.

She flushed a faint pink, and clicked the ball-point pen a second time. "We keep to a strict routine here," she went on, hiding her confusion behind a businesslike air. "I've been on Scarp for more than two years, and during that period we've had hardly any trouble. Nigel, you must bear in mind, isn't a raving maniac. He's usually very rational—as normal as you or I. What's most important is to maintain a peaceful and relaxed atmosphere. Tensions are to be avoided. Excitement is the thing that sets him off."

He took a last drag on his cigarette and snuffed it out in the abalone shell ashtray. "That's how it is with excitement, I guess. But don't worry, I'm a relaxed type. My uncle says we only get every other weekend off. Is that right?"

"Yes, but you're free for four days. It has to be that way, I'm afraid, if we're both to have Saturdays and Sundays on the mainland."

6

"Ten straight days of work—that's a long stretch."

The nurse tossed the pen on the desk and rose from the swivel chair. "You'll get used to it," she said bluntly. "If it will make it any easier for you though, you can have the first weekend."

"Hey, thanks," he responded, delighted. "I can sure use it. Got a lot of unfinished business to take care of in Providence."

"I'll show you your room," she said.

Scarp Island is oval shaped. Since its principal topographical feature is a low hill that extends its length—a distance of less than a third of a mile—it vaguely resembles a half-submerged gray egg floating in the middle of the bay. The West Cottage, a two-storied white-brick building with a terra-cotta pantiled roof, was situated halfway up the hill on the western or landward side. The ground floor of this small building contained the nurse's office and apartment, while the quarters of Osgood and Nigel were on the floor above.

Swinging his suitcase boyishly, Osgood followed Miss Danziger up the stairs to a broad landing. From this they entered a good-sized room—clean, sunny, and comfortable looking. It was equipped with a kitchenette, a modern bathroom, a fireplace, and a relatively new television set.

"The view is quite pleasant, don't you think?" she asked, indicating with a nod of her head the dimity-curtained window between the large chest of drawers and the massive walnut armoire.

Osgood heaved his bag onto the bed, strolled to the window, and stared at the brow of the hill where the mainhouse, Grayhaven, sprawled—a bulky, fourteen-room structure of fieldstone, flanked by numerous sheds and outbuildings that had long since been bleached to a uniform sickly pallor by the sea wind and the salt spray. On the far right a greenhouse with a peaked roof clung to a shoulder of the high ground, its panes scintillating like diamond facets in the bright sunlight.

"Very pretty," he commented without enthusiasm.

They returned to the landing and then made their way through a storeroom stacked with canned goods and other provisions.

"Our evening meals come down from Grayhaven," she explained, "but breakfast and lunch we prepare ourselves. When the Muldoons go ashore, which they don't do very often, we're completely on our own. She's the cook and he's the handyman."

Leaving the pantry they entered a carpeted corridor with two windows in its right-hand wall and two doors in its left. A kneehole desk with a green blotter stood midway down this passage against the outer wall. Both doors were made of solid oak and stained a golden hue, and both were secured by huge iron locks of the sort Osgood associated with medieval dungeons. At eye level each of these imposing portals had a horizontal aperture some fifteen inches wide and two feet in length, the bottom of which had been extended to make a little shelf. A pair of sturdy steel bars traversed these openings from one side to the other.

They stopped at the first door and from a distance of almost a yard looked into the room beyond. The lunatic was clearly visible, but he was sound asleep on a tubular-framed bed whose legs were bolted to the floor. Osgood was surprised to see that he didn't at all resemble his brother. Richard had a ruddy complexion; Nigel's was pale. Richard had a square, slightly jowly face; Nigel's was hollow cheeked and triangular. Richard's hair was smartly cut and nearly as brown as Miss Danziger's; Nigel's was unevenly cropped and the color of asphalt.

Ugly-looking character, the youth thought to himself. That hair doesn't even seem real. It's like the fur of an animal—like a cat skin. And what a pointed chin he has.

When the sleeper grunted and moved one of his

arms, Osgood noticed that his hands were strange, too. Open and with the palms down, they rested limply on the light blue blanket like dead creatures from an alien planet. The thumbs were normal enough, but the rest of the fingers were bizarre. They were all virtually the same size. The long pinkies were especially grotesque.

Miss Danziger drew him away from the door and they returned silently to the staircase landing. "Occasionally he sleeps late," she explained, "and I don't like to awaken him. When you're on duty you'll be sitting at that desk. If he's in a sociable mood, talk to him. If he isn't, don't. It's the wisest course, I've found."

"Does he wear a toupee?" Osgood asked, grinning.

"No. He cuts his hair himself—once a month. Always make sure you get the scissors back from him afterwards. He's usually cooperative because he doesn't want to lose any of his privileges. Before I came he wasn't allowed to cut his hair. When he got too shaggy they had a man come from Providence to do it."

Putting her hands in the white-trimmed pockets of her dress, the nurse then described the security arrangements. Nigel's apartment consisted of a living room and a bedroom. The whole place was lined with concrete, so there was no danger of his setting fire to the cottage. Everything in the apartment was designed with safety in mind—the lights, the sink, the hot plate, the fan, the refrigerator, the shower, the toilet, the heat and ventilation registers. Wherever possible they were recessed and covered by steel grates. There were no long electric wires, no potentially lethal knobs, handles or protruding pipes, no metal towel racks, curtain rods or coat hangers, and no springs in the bed or easy chair. The furniture was fastened to the floor. He used plastic cutlery and plastic cups and dishes, though he did have a light aluminum frying pan and three pots of the same material.

"He takes care of himself for the most part—cooks his breakfast and lunch, washes his dishes, makes his bed, even rinses out his socks," she said. "Once a week we vacuum the apartment and change the linen, and to do this we close the sliding door between the rooms, which operates electrically. If he's on the bedroom side, we clean the living room; if he's in the living room, we do the bedroom. Since he likes things tidy, he never objects to being shunted back and forth. The same key locks both main doors. It's a big intricate iron thing because the locks are especially sturdy and complicated, and it's kept on a hook in a corner of the pantry. You must never, ever, leave the key out in the open anywhere—on the desk, for instance."

"Why?" asked Osgood, leaning indolently on the balustrade.

"Because he has these long tubes that he makes from sheets of newspaper, and with them he can knock articles off the desk, poke them along to the foot of the door, and pick them up with loops of string. Nigel's nothing if not clever."

"How could he reach the lock, though? It's way down the door from the opening. He'd need arms like a gorilla, Miss Danziger."

She assumed a sage expression. "Imprisoned people have plenty of time to scheme. He'd find a method," she said. "Mr. Vaughan has a duplicate key that he keeps in the den at Grayhaven, which we can use if ours ever gets misplaced. When Nigel isn't in sight, you must never stand too near the opening. That's how Mr. MacKenzie got caught. He put his hand inside to take a dish from the shelf, and Nigel was crouching at the bottom of the door. They used to have a piece of mesh over the grill, but they had to remove it because Nigel raised a ruckus about it. He insisted it hampered ventilation. Do you have any questions?"

"Only one," said Osgood with a winsome smile. "Must I always call you Miss Danziger?"

Her eyelashes flickered, yet she met his gaze and

answered, "My name is Adriana. Call me that, if you like."

"Okay. I will. Mine's Edward—but my close friends call me Ned. We'll get along fine, Adriana. I'm sure of it."

"Better unpack your suitcase," she remarked, turning to descend the stairs.

· 2 ·

An hour later, when the nurse knocked at his door, Osgood noticed immediately that she had done something to her eyes—added shadow to the lids or darkened the lashes. Also, there was a touch of red on her cheeks that hadn't been there earlier.

Together they went again to the other side of the cottage. Nigel Vaughan was up and dressed and sitting on the edge of his cot reading *The New York Times*. But when Adriana called to him and tried to introduce Osgood, he obstinately refused to acknowledge their presence. A tall man with sloping shoulders and muscular arms, he wore a knit shirt and straight-legged denim jeans. His eyes were such an extremely light blue that at first glance he appeared walleyed. The girl cajoled him and pleaded with him, but he never once raised those eyes from the pages of his newspaper. At last she gave up and went off to the mainhouse on an errand, leaving Osgood at the desk to perform his inaugural tour of duty.

For fifteen or twenty minutes the new attendant sat quietly in the corridor thumbing through an old copy of *Newsweek*, and during this period all was tranquil. Then suddenly he heard a low, harsh, rumbling noise like the growling of a large and discontented dog. He got up and peered through the bars from a safe distance. Nigel was no longer reading his paper. Instead he was standing on the far side of the room wagging his head like a metronome, drooling copiously, shuffling his bare feet, and making herky-jerk gestures with his peculiar hands like an angry mute. The rumbling came from deep in his chest. It had a hollow reverberant quality that was eerie and irritating.

"For cripes sake!" Osgood exclaimed in alarm. "What's wrong, Nigel? What the hell's the matter?"

The lunatic, however, seemed totally incapable of providing this information, and only rolled his head, shuffled his feet, and growled all the louder. Convinced he was witnessing a seizure, the youth got on the phone and called Grayhaven.

"Nothing to worry about," Adriana said serenely, after he had described what was happening. "Nigel's just upset by your arrival. To him it's a great event—one that he's afraid will mean changes in the routine of his life, I suppose. You must remember, too, he never meets strangers. But pay no attention to his antics, Edward, and he'll soon grow tired of acting like an imbecile."

Relieved by her assurances, Osgood hung up and did his best to disregard the commotion emanating from behind the golden oak door. It was an effort that failed miserably, though. The sounds were simply too outlandish, too distracting. When Nigel finished growling,he began to bray like a donkey. By the time this cacophonous performance ended, the young man had a throbbing headache. Ten minutes of bovine lowing, another ten of ovine bleating, and a seemingly interminable stretch of porcine grunting shattered him completely. Unable to endure any more he fled to his room, gulped two aspirin, and lay down on his bed.

A half-hour later, feeling slightly better, Osgood returned to the corridor. All was peace and quiet. Except for the droning of an electric fan, there wasn't a sound. He looked through the aperture of the first door, but Nigel wasn't in the bedroom. Then he looked through the second door and saw the lunatic seated in his easy chair. He had stopped slavering and grimacing and was reading a paperback book. On the table in front of him was a cinnamon doughnut and a plastic mug of what appeared to be cocoa. With his long legs crossed and his feet shod in a pair of gray felt slippers, he might have been any normal solid citizen relaxing in the homey comfort of his suburban parlor.

"Hello, Edward," Nigel said, without lifting his eyes.

"Hello, Nigel," Osgood answered, astonished but delighted by this swift change in behaviour. "Feeling okay?"

"I'm very well, thank you," came the reply. A brief pause ensued, after which he added, "In spite of that wretched bird this morning."

"Bird?"

"Bird."

"What bird was that, Nigel?"

"The one that awoke me at dawn—a starling, I think. I had an awful time falling back to sleep again. That's why I got up so late. Perhaps it was a grackle, the little fiend. Kept hopping around on the window ledge like a thing on wires."

"Oh. That must have been pretty annoying."

"I'll say it was." Nigel flipped a page, drank some cocoa and blinked his light blue eyes. "It whistled, too—whistled, whistled, whistled. Most unusual—extraordinary, in fact."

In a soothing tone, Osgood asked, "Extraordinary, Nigel? Why do you think a bird's whistling is extraordinary?"

"What?"

"I mean starlings whistle all the time, don't they?"

"True," the man in the easy chair conceded readily, "but this particular starling was whistling 'Caro nome' from *Rigoletto*. I call that damned curious, don't you?"

Osgood grinned. "I guess so," he said.

"I'll bet you don't even know when arias are supposed to be sung—do you, Edward?"

"Arias? Is it some kind of riddle? I give up, if it is."

13

With his oddly shaped hand, Nigel patted the coarse black hair on the crown of his head, and replied triumphantly, "Arias must be sung at opera-tune moments. Ha, ha! How old are you?"

"Twenty-five," the attendant answered, looking more than a little confused as he leaned on the sill of the barred opening.

"That's young. I'm forty-five. It seems only a few months since I was a stripling, measuring the world with wide and innocent eyes. I discovered it's a rather ghastly place, the world. I went to your mother's wedding in Kingston. Her name is Elizabeth. She was a stunning bride, with delicate features and dimples in her cheeks."

"My mother is still a good-looking woman," Osgood said proudly. "Still pretty, still young."

"I'm delighted to hear it, Edward. Beauty so seldom endures. My own mother died of acute alcoholism when I was eight. Her name was Victoria. Each day she consumed three quarts of Gordon's gin, regular as clockwork. The house, cellar to attic, reeked of juniper. The word gin is derived from the French *genièvre*, which means juniper. The drink itself was invented by a Dutch druggist. Don't care for it personally, but they say Hazlitt loved the stuff. I never saw my mother sober. To me she was always a disheveled woman in a pink or fuchsia peignoir; a sad creature with bleary eyes, mulberry-red complexion, nicotine-stained fingers, and a voice like the rasp of a rusty hinge."

Nigel gazed up at his companion and the corners of his mouth curled slightly, giving his wedge of a face a sardonic cast.

Osgood, uncertain of how to respond to these remarks, said after a moment, "Liquor ruins a lot of people's lives, I guess."

From outside the faint chugging of a distant motorboat floated into the cottage.

"Well, well, so you're Elizabeth's son," the prisoner

declared jauntily. "There hasn't been much contact between our families of late, I'm afraid. Your father, James, was my first cousin. He once treated me to a baseball game in Pawtucket, and crammed me with hot dogs and orange tonic. I've always been partial to orange tonic. I love the color of it even more than the taste. Richard told me your father died, and I was grieved to hear it. We lost touch with everybody after my father got elected to congress. Wealth and power often make people standoffish—foolish people, at any rate. He was a blackguard, my father—a fraud, a crook, a mountebank."

Embarrassed, Osgood made no reply. The throbbing of the motorboat grew louder, sounding sullen and querulous. Nigel had another mouthful of his cocoa, uncrossed his legs and said, "I'm reading a book on teacup fortune-telling, but it's a load of nonsense. I myself don't even drink tea. What is it but a pile of dead leaves boiled in water? Sometimes flower petals are put in tea. Were you aware of that? Hot chocolate or coffee are more to my taste. The Russians drink fermented tea, according to a pamphlet Adriana brought me. Whenever she goes ashore she hunts up things for me to read—books on quaint subjects. Yesterday I read one on the cutting of silhouettes, and the day before I finished a life of Alexander the Great by a Fordham Jesuit. Old, small, hardcover books are the best. I've got a nifty little volume—a dissertation on Roman antiquities, published in London in 1877—saved for tomorrow. Did you know Alexander the Great couldn't swim? It hardly seems possible, does it? I can't swim either, not a stroke. Neither can Adriana. She's a sweet girl, don't you agree?"

"Yes," said Osgood. "But she's kind of old for a girl, isn't she?"

"I don't think so, Edward."

"How old would you say she is, Nigel? Twenty-eight?"

"I have no idea. Why don't you ask her, eh? Strange

15

how water affects different people. My brother took to it right away. Toss him in the ocean and he'd cavort like a dolphin. But me? Once I feel myself in deep water I become petrified with terror. Perhaps poor Alexander, brave as he was, reacted similarly. Courage comes in many forms. A man who's afraid of cockroaches might be perfectly willing to wrestle a twenty-foot crocodile. Did you know the people of the Irrawaddy delta eat crocodiles? It's true. They catch them with a hook and line, using a duck or a puppy for bait. Reminds me of the old joke: 'Give me a crocodile sandwich, and make it snappy.' Ha, ha! Can you swim, Edward?"

"Yes," he answered, his mind in a whirl at Nigel's rapid changes of topic. "I'm pretty good at it, in fact."

"You're lucky. My inability to cope with water is the main reason Richard imprisoned me on this wretched island—like Edmond Dantès, the Count of Monte Cristo. Or Dr. Mudd. Or Napoleon Bonaparte, for that matter. Even if I break out, which I did once by pulling the pins out of the door hinges with a coat hanger, my chances of escaping are slim. They keep the small boats chained and padlocked, as I soon discovered when I got there that night. Then MacKenzie and two fellows from the mainland grabbed me and carried me back bodily. Afterwards, Richard had a machinist redesign the hinges, and that was that. But he would have found a way."

Baffled, Osgood asked, "Who?"

"Alexander the Great, naturally. It was said of him that his perspiration had an agreeable odor. Isn't that remarkable? Mine doesn't smell agreeable, not even to me. Do you realize he was only twenty-five—your age, Edward—when he conquered Darius at Guagamela and so became ruler of the whole Persian Empire? Yes, a mere twenty-five. Still, he was afraid of deep ponds and rolling rivers, of a few cubic yards of Adam's ale."

"Wasn't Alexander the Great's father a king? I think I saw a movie about him once."

"Yes, yes. Fancy your knowing that! There's really nothing like a classical education, is there? Alexander's dad was Philip of Macedon, a very powerful king indeed."

Smiling unevenly, Osgood said, "If my father had been rich and powerful, maybe at the age of twenty-five I'd be a conqueror, too."

"Excellent, Edward! Ha, ha! A charming notion. Maybe you'd be trudging through the Punjab this very moment. But I had a father who was rich and powerful, and look where I am. Oh, you'd make a fine warlord, I'm sure. And you know how to swim, too. I wonder if Alexander had other phobias. A boy at prep school, James Bresnahan, was terrified of venetian blinds. I myself can't tolerate loud noises—roaring airplanes, boisterous crowds, clamorous music. Has Adriana explained how irritable such things make me?"

"Uncle Richard mentioned it."

"Uncle Richard? You mean my brother. I suppose in a sense he's . . ." Nigel stopped abruptly and inclined his head. "I do believe that boat's coming to Scarp," he declared softly, as though to himself. Flinging the paperback on the lucite table, he jumped to his feet and hurried to the window. "Yes—it's Flowers' launch, all right. And...and Louise is there in the bow." His voice quavered with excitement. From a pocket of his jeans he yanked a small pair of opera glasses, raised them to his eyes, and exclaimed, "She's like Cleopatra on her barge or Scheherazade on a dhow. I'm so glad to see you again, Louise dear. What a pity she can't hear me! Louise, I'd kiss the ground for you. I would, and with the greatest of pleasure. Doesn't she look superb in that striped Basque shirt? And she's tinted her hair a bit, I think. Elevate your eyes, darling girl. Favor me with a limpid glance. How trim and graceful she is!"

Puzzled, Osgood knit his brow and asked, "Who's Louise?"

17

But Nigel, wholly occupied by the scene below, refused to answer the question, though it was put to him several times.

· 3 ·

Mrs. Muldoon, a chubby blunt-faced woman with mouse-gray hair, was deaf as a brick, as was her husband. She gave Osgood the two full hand-baskets, and he left the huge modern kitchen of the mainhouse and went back out into the dazzling sunlight.

Not bad, he thought as he walked down the flagstone path, feeling the heat penetrate the flesh of his bare arms and legs. In a week I'll be as tanned as a lifeguard. There are worse ways to live than this. And the job has interesting possibilities, too.

As he neared the corner of the house a voice called to him from the screened-in porch, interrupting his reverie. An instant later a short, frail, red-haired man in a somber charcoal business suit emerged from the shadowy interior and came sauntering towards him.

"You're Edward Osgood, aren't you?" he inquired, a meager smile on his pink lips. "Thought I'd introduce myself. I'm Leon Perth, Mr. Vaughan's personal secretary."

"Hi. Nice meeting you," Osgood replied, setting one of the baskets on the ground and offering the man his hand, which was accepted, clasped in a feeble grip, and quickly released.

"You arrived yesterday, I understand," said Perth, squinting his eyes against the solar glare. "How do you like the place?"

"I think it's great. Fresh air, perfect weather, private beaches—you can't do much better than that, can you?"

"I guess not. But in the winter the island undergoes a drastic change, you know—an incredible metamorphosis. The cold wind comes off the ocean like a scythe, and everything gets very, very bleak. What's your opinion of Nigel? Do you think him great, too?"

"To tell the truth, he's not as bad as I thought he'd be," Osgood said. "I figure I'll manage him all right. Even though I'm not really a nurse, I've always been pretty adaptable. He's kind of comical, isn't he?"

"In a macabre sort of way," Perth agreed, nodding his red head. "Remember, however, Nigel's a psychopath and extremely dangerous. In him you see the strength of a gorilla combined with the mind of an autistic child."

"He's weird all right. But I don't worry about physical situations, Leon, because I can handle myself in a tussle. I'm not what you'd call a weakling."

These smug statements by Osgood caused the secretary—who was less than five and a half feet tall and had the bone structure of a twelve-year-old boy—to bridle noticeably. "Perhaps not, Edward," he answered. "Still you would never, never be a match for Nigel. He's a savage, a brute, a monster—and very cunning. Heed my words, or one day you'll be sorry."

"Okay, I'll keep it in mind."

Jamming his hands into his trouser pockets, the little man peered up at Osgood who towered almost eight inches above him and, adopting a tone that was distinctly haughty, declared, "I trust you've been given proper and detailed instructions. Reticence and discretion are essential. In view of Mr. Vaughan's prominence in public affairs, we do everything in our power to keep his personal life as private as possible. Many years ago Nigel gave an interview to a newspaper reporter that caused a good deal of trouble, and we don't want that to happen again. Not ever. He'll tell you a lot of rubbish, too, but never repeat what he says to outsiders. Even the Muldoons shouldn't be taken into your confidence, since they probably wouldn't remain with us long if they knew just how crazy our Nigel really is. Discretion is vital. Do you understand, Edward?"

19

"I sure do, Leon. You're the third person to warn me about that," said Osgood, grinning impudently.

"It can't be mentioned too often. You'll find Adriana quite competent. Do you like her?"

"She seems fine. I think we'll get along okay."

"Nigel's fond of her. No grand passion, of course— he's too gaga for that—but there does seem to be a curious bond of affection between them. Personally I find Nigel about as attractive as a rabid dog. However, there's no accounting for taste, is there? It's a small cottage. I hope you won't get in each other's way down there. But, as you're so adaptable, I don't imagine that will be a problem." The secretary sniggered and just perceptibly winked his eye. Then, withdrawing his hands from his pockets, he said, "I mustn't keep you, though. You'll have your chores to tend to."

He turned and walked back up the hill, looking strangely out of place against the bright blue sky.

Osgood retrieved his basket and resumed his journey.

The provisions were divided into three allotments, one for each of them.

"The ice cream is mushy," Adriana remarked.

"It must have melted while I was talking to Leon Perth," Osgood told her. "I met him outside the house, and got some more instructions on how to handle Nigel."

"From Leon?" She laughed. "He knows nothing about Nigel. Hasn't seen him for at least a year. They don't get along. Nigel detests him."

"I wonder why," he said, grinning.

"Oh, don't let Leon bother you, Edward. He just likes to chatter and act important," said Adriana, carrying the half-gallon tub of ice cream to the refrigerator. "I'll keep this down here because it won't fit in your freezer compartment, but anytime you want it come in and help yourself."

20

"Okay," Osgood said, glancing at her covertly. Then he added, "I'd better take the stuff for me and Nigel upstairs, or the butter will be melting, too."

· 4 ·

"No, I never related that tale to you before," Nigel said, his faded blue eyes indignant. "You're confusing it with my flight from the Selkirk Sanitarium, when I leaped out the dining room window into the copper beech tree and nearly broke my leg. Or maybe you're thinking of my glorious escape from Rose Hill Manor in California—the time I tore up the floorboards and kicked a hole in the ceiling plaster to get down to the lobby, then hitched a ride to San Francisco on the motorcycle. No, Adriana, this is an entirely different one. I'm positive I've never told you this story—never revealed how I stole those raincoats, for instance. The used-clothing dealer, a bald-headed Polish man with a face as long as a bloodhound's, paid me a hundred and twenty dollars for them, which surprised me greatly. He already had dozens of similar coats on his pipe-racks. When I walked in, I felt like a collier bringing coals to Newcastle. Have you ever wondered about the word 'Newcastle'? If the English insist on saying fo'c'sle for forecastle, it seems to me they should say Newc'sle for Newcastle. No wonder the language is in such a state. But then, Emerson felt consistency was the hobgoblin of little minds, didn't he? What a Pandora's box that opens! All profundities are pitfalls, I suspect."

He popped the last of the sandwich in his mouth and chewed it slowly, his triangular face framed in the opening.

Adriana ran the needle through the button and the cloth and pulled the thread taut on the other side. The shirt was spread out on the desk before her, empty arms extended as if in entreaty.

21

"But they caught you again," she said complacently, "so what did you gain by it all?"

Nigel arched his eyebrows, creating a network of creases that went right up to the margin of his dark furry coiffure. "Are you serious?" he asked. "What did I gain? Why, I gained three whole days of liberty, Adriana—three of the merriest days of my life. I dined in a French restaurant, I went to a Turkish bath, I bought a mechanical pencil that wrote in four different colors, I watched a Little League game, I ate about a dozen Hershey bars, I went to a theater and saw an Italian movie with subtitles, I had coffee and eclairs at a tea shop, I spent hours looking at all the new automobiles rush down the eight-lane highway, and I visited the zoo. I also bought myself a nifty coconut straw hat with a pugaree band, and a pair of orange socks. Did you know that orange was Charles Dickens' favorite color, too?"

"No," Adriana said. "Was it?"

"Absolutely. I read it in his biography," Nigel replied, wiping his mouth with a paper napkin. "My downfall, like that of so many others in this dismal world, was drink. On the afternoon of the third day I decided that a dram of rye whiskey wouldn't do me any harm—a rash decision if ever there was one. Isn't it astonishing how alcohol bemuses the brain? The first glass led to a second, and the second to a third. Within a couple of hours I consumed roughly a jeroboam of the wretched fluid. Then an ignoramus in a paisley shirt started playing the jukebox and a scuffle developed. The next thing I knew I was on the barroom floor looking up at a massive state trooper. He wore steel-rimmed sunglasses, jodhpurs, and shiny leather leggings, and his wide belt was festooned with lethal weapons and other vital gadgets: a billy club, a ring of keys, handcuffs, a two-way radio, a book of summonses, a whistle, a case full of fountain pens, an ivory-handled revolver, and a bloodcurdling array of .38 caliber cartridges. The fellow was ready to take on a herd of rogue

elephants. I didn't stand a chance, Adriana. They pum-
meled me a bit, hauled me out of the bar, and threw me
bodily into a Black Maria—and that, alas, was the end of
my furlough. Nevertheless I did enjoy three days of unfettered freedom and, believe me, three days of unfettered
freedom are worth a fractured jaw, a dislodged bicuspid, a
sore rib cage, a broken metatarsus, and a few tender
lumps on the old cranium. Every rose has its thorns, eh?
The only real regret I had was that I lost my straw hat and
the mechanical pencil that wrote in four different colors."

The nurse smiled and shook her curly head. "I don't
know why you can't come to terms with the world, Nigel,"
she said.

The lunatic rolled the paper napkin into a tight ball
and flicked it through the bars. It described a shallow arc
and landed in the wastebasket beside the desk. "Perhaps
I can now," he said. "Lately I'm much more relaxed . . .
more even-tempered . . . more settled. Haven't you
noticed? I attribute it to your tranquil influence, my im-
perturbable Adriana. I daresay that if I were given another chance, I could live like a normal human being. Yes,
I'm certain I could."

Having completed her sewing job, the young woman
snipped the thread with her teeth, tested the button by
giving it a tug, and then proceeded to fold the shirt into a
neat rectangle. "For a time I did think you were improv-
ing, Nigel," she said gently, "but that was before you
injured Mr. MacKenzie."

Nigel's face became sullen. "MacKenzie provoked
me—you know that," he muttered. "MacKenzie took
pleasure in baiting me."

"Yes, he did. Still, people with healthy minds don't
resort to violence in such situations."

"But they do . . . they do. It happens constantly.
Don't you read the newspapers?" He halted suddenly, as
though fearful of saying too much, and when he spoke
again his voice was devoid of emotion. "If I became angry

that day, it was because I'm under a strain, Adriana. An imprisoned man is a coiled spring. If I were free, I'd be a different person. Captives are like steam in a boiler—highly volatile. Once they're released, however, the pressure is dissipated immediately." Nigel drew closer to the opening and rubbed his nose on the bars. "There were other reasons for my . . . irresponsible action, too. Remember, I'm undergoing a continuous and interminable punishment—and, since I can't suffer more than I'm suffering already, there isn't much reason for me to be law-abiding. I hurt MacKenzie because I could do so with impunity. Who wouldn't avenge himself on his enemies, knowing he couldn't be called to account for it? Even you, sweet Adriana, might commit a crime under those lenient circumstances."

"I have no enemies," she answered, regarding him with frank brown eyes.

"Perhaps not, but you're still young. We don't know what the future holds in store for you, do we?" Nigel smiled disarmingly. "All I'm saying is that I wouldn't do abnormal things if I were allowed to lead a normal life. Fundamentally, I'm a rather easygoing individual, and with age I'm becoming even more mellow. Why don't you leave that key on the desk for me some night—eh, Adriana? And unlock one of those rowboats in the shed? I give you my solemn word that once I get away, I'll never hurt another person as long as I live."

"You can't make such a promise, Nigel. Besides, you know perfectly well that it would be wrong of me to release you."

"I'm not asking you to, am I? I'm asking only a small favor: that you make a mistake, that you forget to hang the damned key in the pantry. A little mental lapse is all I require, and a bit of carelessness in the boathouse. No one will blame you."

"Your brother is in charge here," the nurse replied obstinately. "Whether you're set free or not is up to him."

"My brother is evil. You've been on Scarp long enough to appreciate that. He wouldn't release me if the building was on fire. No, Adriana, you're making excuses for yourself—rationalizing. The responsibility is yours and yours alone, because you're my only friend, my only comfort, my only hope."

"I wouldn't dare do it. You're dangerous."

"Nonsense, I've become as mild as a suckling lamb."

"It would be a betrayal of your brother's trust."

"What a pity your loyalty isn't attached to a better cause. Tyrants owe their power to wishy-washy creatures like you. But I won't remain here and rot. Never, never, never. I'll bust out on my own. Mark my words, I'll flee this blasted island as sure as Daedalus fled Crete. In the end I'll defeat my brother—crush him under my heel. Wait and see. There are more ways to skin a cat than to drag him through a keyhole on a piece of string."

Adriana calmly picked up a second shirt, examined it for missing buttons, dropped it in her lap, and began rethreading the needle. "If you did escape, and I don't for a minute think you can, you wouldn't be able to see Louise any more. Have you thought about that?"

"Yes, I have. I think about everything. What's to stop me from going to Newport, to her condominium?"

"The police, I should imagine," said Adriana, taking a white button from a small tin box and matching it against those on the shirt. "Didn't she call them the last time you visited her?"

"No, she didn't," the lunatic retorted, annoyed. "The night clerk at that hotel, and the house detective—they were the cause of that ridiculous furor. The two of them assaulted me. Louise was asleep, which was why I banged on the door."

"They testified that you splintered the panel, Mac-Kenzie told me, and that you had a breadknife in your belt."

"All lies. A breadknife? Hah! A pitiful little thing, it

25

was hardly more than a nail file, Adriana. And, as I informed that senile judge, I only brought it with me because it was late at night, and the downtown area was alive with footpads and muggers. In any case, Louise wasn't the one who turned me in. If I got away from here, I'd probably see more of her rather than less."

Some faint strains of music drifted into the corridor, then ceased abruptly as though a door had been closed on them.

"Does his radio bother you?" she asked.

"No, I rarely hear it. But he's been after me to let him bring it out here to the desk. Says he has earphones, so it wouldn't disturb me. Why are people so fond of music, I wonder? To me, kind hearts are better than clarinets. Or castanets, for that matter. I suppose I'll let him, though, if he treats me decently. What do you think of the boy, anyway?"

"Edward? He's very nice," she answered in a voice that was excessively casual.

"I myself find him a bit looney. He calls Richard his uncle. I don't know much about the degrees of consanguinity, but I'm certain your father's cousin isn't your uncle. Moreover, if Richard was his uncle I'd be his uncle too, yet he doesn't call me Uncle Nigel. I suspect he's ambitious. He told me that if his father had been well off, he himself would've been another Alexander the Great. Can you imagine such conceit? Delusions of grandeur. He'll be acting like Napoleon next. Have you noticed his eyes, Adriana? They're weird—big and dark, like a nocturnal animal's. Yes, just like a kinkajou's or a tarsier's or a Euphrates jerboa's. Or perhaps a grand galago's or a douroucouli's. He's a primitive type, and probably not entirely stable. I suppose he thinks he can get rich and powerful by hanging around Richard, but if he does he's in for a shock. My brother's a taker, not a giver. When we were boys, he always swindled me out of my allowance—and he didn't really need the money, either. Did it

26

out of sheer perversity and greed. James Osgood, Edward's father, was a very generous fellow, which is why he ended up as he did. Never had two nickels to rub together in his pocket. Had to use one nickel and a button. Ha, ha! That's an old college joke. You like Edward, though, don't you. Maybe he has virtues I've yet to discover. Every clod is liable to have a silver lining, eh? Ha, ha!" Nigel scratched his furry poll, then yawned behind a long-fingered hand. "I'll manage, I guess, as long as you're here. But if you left I don't know what would happen to me. In all likelihood I'd go crazy. Can you find me a book on dream interpretation?"

"I think so," she said.

"Last night I dreamt I was a feather duster. Have you ever dreamt you were a feather duster? Or a whisk broom or hairbrush or something similar?"

Adriana looked up at him with a twinkle in her eyes. "No, Nigel. What's it like, being a feather duster?" she asked.

"Surprisingly disagreeable. I felt humiliated, mortified. I felt as if I were the victim of a monstrous injustice. I felt quite abased. I felt that the whole universe had conspired against me. And then, after awhile, I became obsessed with the idea of revenge. I wanted to demolish the world—bring it all down." The lunatic smiled. "That's comical, isn't it? A feather duster wanting to bring the world down. Ha, ha! How much down can there be in a feather duster?"

With this last quip, he left the opening and wandered back to his bedroom, chuckling softly.

Adriana finished her work and set both shirts on the shelf of the oaken door. Then she fell to daydreaming of Edward Osgood.

· 5 ·

From the patch pocket of his lime-green cotton-gabardine jacket, Richard Vaughan dug a monogrammed silver case, flicked it open, and helped himself to a slender, tawny cigar without offering one to Osgood. "I do my best to make his life easier," he said in a resonant voice, "but it's a frustrating business. Despite my efforts he remains sick and miserable. And he doesn't like me, Edward, which complicates the problem." Vaughan slipped the case back in his pocket, thrust the cigar between his even teeth, lit it with a silver lighter, and took several quick puffs. "But what can't be cured, must be endured," he added, an expression of martyrdom on his ruddy face.

Osgood nodded and said deferentially, "It must be hard to have to worry about him all the time—especially for a person as busy as you are, Uncle Richard."

"Edward, you have no idea. Still, one can't shirk one's duties," the politician answered patly, smoke wreathing the crown of his head like a halo. "The worst of it is, people inevitably feel guilty when a member of their family is mentally ill. Of course the psychiatrists say this is natural, but that doesn't help much—doesn't help much at all. You keep recalling the past, searching for the root of the tragedy. You delve and brood. You endlessly analyze. Old, old scenes in old, old settings haunt you like specters from the grave. Minor details of past events suddenly assume an awful significance. You ponder the things you've done, and those you've failed to do. You relive ancient conversations, regretting what was said and what was left unspoken. That's how it is. Just now, Nigel and I had an argument about some silly incident that occurred twenty-five years ago. For him, though, it was a vivid as if it had happened yesterday. We're both of us locked up in a moldy labyrinth of bitter memories."

With eyes of a much darker blue than his brother's, Vaughan gazed vacantly past the corner of the cottage to the jetty, where Jack Flowers and Henry Coombs were struggling with a stiff tarpaulin on the deck of the *Monica-Mae.* "How different it might have been!" he said feelingly. "Together, Nigel and I could have performed titanic deeds. With one of us in Providence and the other on the Potomac, we would have had a real power base. In politics, families have a tremendous advantage. The Lodges, the Longs, the Kennedys, the Tafts—they were people to reckon with. But for the Vaughans, alas, it wasn't meant to be. I must struggle on alone. Instead of being supported by a faithful ally, I'm burdened with an endless responsibility. Yet what choice have I? Nigel and I are linked by blood, by psychic and physical bonds that only death can sever. Still, though we were born of the same mother and father, we aren't friends. A strange unnatural antagonism separated us even as children—a broad gulf that neither of us could bridge. He never understood my views, nor I his. It was because we were both strong willed, I suppose, and passionate in our beliefs. Each of us had a quick and violent temper, too, which didn't help matters. An affiliation exists between love and hatred. They're near relatives—like brothers."

Made ill at ease by these personal revelations, Osgood shuffled his feet and smiled tentatively. Upstairs Adriana began vacuuming the hall; the banshee howl of the machine came down to them in nagging waves. Had the nurse been present during the meeting of the two men? he wondered. Had she heard their argument?

Aware at last that he had to make some contribution to the conversation, the youth said, "Nigel's a very intelligent person. He knows about everything. I guess he's read a ton of books."

Richard Vaughan tapped ash from the slim cigar. "An omnivorous reader, he was. At fifteen he graduated from Lyle, and would have gone straight to Harvard if he hadn't suffered that first nervous attack. Used to sit for hours on end, consuming huge volumes: *Moby Dick*, Boswell's *Life of Johnson*, *Don Quixote*, *Plutarch's Lives*, *Les Misérables*. Nigel actually finished the whole *Decline and Fall of the Roman Empire*, believe it or not—a thing that's twice as long as the Bible. But it was all this learning that eventually unhinged his mind, Edward. He got lost in a wilderness of words and speculations. The voices of those great authors combined in a siren song that lured my poor brother to disaster. Profound ideas can be treacherous. I remember an Easter vacation here on Scarp, when I had to study thirty pages of Plato for a philosophy course and, incredible as it may seem, by the time I finished poring over those devious dialogues my mind was in such a turmoil that I couldn't get a wink of sleep that entire night."

Osgood assumed a sympathetic look, but didn't speak.

The politician went on in his rich, lyrical baritone. "Excessive learning, like any other excess, is harmful. Nigel overindulged. He gorged himself on abstractions—logic, ethics, and that sort of thing. The weight of it all crushed his brain. It's rather like the opera, *Faust*, where the man comes to grief because he tried to possess too much wisdom. I've noticed now that my brother reads only pamphlets—small books dealing with trifling subjects—as though he's finally realized the peril that lurks in the products of genius. For myself, being a public servant, I find men and women and current events far more fascinating than cumbersome biographies and dusty tomes on ancient history. The living are my concern, not the dead. I prefer real people to Oliver Twist or Anna Karenina." He interrupted his discourse to suck on the cigar and blow a cumulous cloud of white smoke into the crystalline air. "Ah, Edward—if only Nigel had been sane. We Vaughans would have ruled the roost, as sure as fire burns. The state of Rhode Island would have been our pocket kingdom. Who knows? We might even have set up a dynasty. There have been presidents of this great country of ours who rose to power under far less favorable circumstances."

His lips tightened in a rudimentary smile, while his shadowy blue eyes stared down towards the jetty. Then he remarked in a lighter tone, "But I must get back to the house—to my den. I'm expecting an important call from Washington. An old friend at H.E.W. is doing me a little favor. Do you think you'll like living here?"

"Oh yes, Uncle Richard. It's a beautiful place . . . and the job is very interesting—a challenge," Osgood replied, almost bowing in his eagerness to show gratitude. "I couldn't be happier."

"Excellent, excellent. You'll find that if you're loyal to me, Edward, I'll be generous to you," the politician declared, waving his cigar magisterially.

Turning, he ascended the hill with dignified step.

Long after his departure Osgood lingered by the cottage door, sniffing with pleasure the pungent tobacco fragrance that his suave employer had left behind.

· 6 ·

A little before midnight Osgood set off for the beach in swimming trunks and a college T-shirt with *Ned O.* stenciled across the back. In the sable heavens a not-quite-full moon hung like a clipped silver coin on a black velvet cloth. Aided by it and the floodlight near the jetty, he had no difficulty in making his way down the winding, gravel-strewn path. A balmy breeze laden with the salty smell of the sea and the subtle aroma of heather and broom stirred the air.

Edward Osgood was a well-built young man—broad of shoulder, full of chest, narrow of hip, and long of leg. Though six feet, two inches tall, his movements were not awkward. His gait possessed all the easy grace of a Zulu or an Iroquois. He had an attractive, evenly proportioned face, large black eyes, and a head of bushy dark brown hair.

Reaching the top of a low bluff that overlooked the shore, he was surprised to see the slender form of a woman scarcely a dozen yards away. She had fair skin and was stark naked. In the moonlight her wet body gleamed like glass. Since the woman was occupied with drying her long blonde hair, she did not at first notice his arrival— and Osgood took full advantage of this circumstance to examine her from head to toe. From her face he judged her to be around thirty-five, but her figure was as lean and small breasted as that of an adolescent girl. Hardly breathing, he watched her with intensity, until finally she turned her head to shake out her damp tresses and spied him looming there.

"Where the hell did you come from?" she asked, startled but by no means frightened. "And why the hell are you gawking at me?"

"I . . . I'm Edward Osgood," he answered, disconcerted. "From the cottage."

"The cottage? Oh yes—looking after Nigel," she said, staring up at him with eyes that were almost as inquisitive as his own. "Richard spoke of you. You're a relative—a second cousin or something, aren't you? But he didn't mention you were a voyeur, too. Put your eyes back in your head, Edward. All that heavy concentration will give you migraine." She returned to shaking out her hair and rubbing her scalp with the towel, making no effort to cover her bare body. "A big boy like you shouldn't still be obsessed with dirty little games."

"I didn't know you were here. I'm sorry," he apologized hastily.

She glanced up at him from under the veil of her blonde locks. "You don't look sorry," she said caustically, "and you're continuing to ogle me. Don't you know that's rude? Whatever can you be thinking of, Edward? Well-bred young men don't ogle strange naked ladies. It's a breach of etiquette, to say the least."

With obvious reluctance, he transferred his gaze to the ocean beyond her, where windrows of white surf were methodically mounting the sloping shore. "Sorry," he declared again.

The woman smiled. "But perhaps you've never seen a naked lady before," she said mischievously, "and you're consumed with curiosity. If that's the case I hope I'm not a disappointment to you. Ladies, despite what you may have heard, are not too different from gentlemen—at least not on the surface. Two arms, two legs, etcetera. Not much to fall into a trance about, dear."

Stung by her remarks, Osgood uttered what was meant to be a sardonic laugh, but it wasn't loud enough to be effective. "I've seen my share of naked women," he said. "Maybe more than my share."

"Really? How thrilling for you! And you're hardly more than a lad. That's what it is to be precocious, though, I guess," she replied in a mocking voice. Finished with her hair, she commenced drying her slim body, running the towel over her flesh in long deliberate strokes. "Why are you down here, anyway?"

"For the same reason you are. I came for a swim."

"A pity you didn't come earlier, Edward," she said, favoring him with another glance and another sly smile. "We might have swum together."

The youth thought about this for a moment, then answered, "You could stay, couldn't you?"

Her laughter was low and soft, like a chord played on a mandolin. "I think not, dear, appealing as the idea is. Besides, you're ravishing me with your eyes again. If you've come to swim, why the hell don't you? The ocean's over there. I'm not planning to do any go-go dances, so you won't be missing an awful lot."

Flinging his towel over his shoulder in a defiant gesture, Osgood started down the incline. "Are you Louise?" he asked, when he reached the bottom.

"I'm Mrs. Vaughan," she said curtly.

"Mrs. Vaughan?" he repeated, suddenly diffident. "I didn't know. I'm sorry, but I never realized Uncle Richard had a wife."

The woman laughed a second time, though it was a

harsher sound than before. "Nothing to be sorry about, nothing at all," she said. "I'm not sensitive about manners really—or morals, either. But why do you call him Uncle Richard? He's not your uncle."

"I don't know, Mrs. Vaughan. It's just a kind of habit. He doesn't seem to mind."

From a leather tote bag at her feet she took a light, sleeveless dress and, without hurrying, slipped it over her head. Pulling it down over her breasts and hips, she said, "Of course he doesn't. Richard's a politician, and politicians try to be agreeable to everybody. That's their big talent. They're professional charmers—handshakers, cheek-patters, baby-kissers."

Osgood detected an acrid note in her voice and a cynical glint in her eyes. With a few deft movements she tied the towel around her hair, winding it into a high turban. He found himself contemplating the pale oval of her neatly shaven armpit, and guiltily looked away.

"I guess you're right," he remarked. "Politicians have to be diplomatic. Well, it's been very nice meeting you, Mrs. Vaughan. I sure hope I didn't bother you."

"You didn't," she answered smoothly. "But even if you did, Edward—we all get bothered on occasion, don't we?"

Then, flashing an ambiguous smile, she stepped into a pair of cork-soled sandals, gathered up her bag, turned, and leisurely ascended the bluff.

The water was tepid. Floating on his back and staring at the wan eccentric moon, he considered his new acquaintance and her parting smile.

"God, she's really transmitting signals," he said under his breath. "I'll bet if I just put my hand on her, I could have had her right there. But I can't mess around. I'd lose the damned job for sure."

During the half-hour he spent paddling about in the sea, Louise Vaughan's nude figure kept flitting in and out

34

of the chambers of his mind, like a white bird trapped in a derelict building.

Emerging from the water at last, he loped up the shingled shore. While he was drying himself he heard a rustling noise in the shrubbery at the bottom of the scarp.

Rats, he thought uneasily.

He dressed as fast as he could and started back. Through the gloom he could distinguish the shadowy bulk of Grayhaven on the summit of the hill. In one window a feeble yellow light shone, like a smuggler's beacon on some wild and desolate coast.

As he neared his destination he noticed a light in Adriana Danziger's window and, entering the cottage, he tapped softly on her door. She opened it almost immediately. She wore a short, cornflower-blue robe of crepe de chine, and a book was in her hand.

"I saw you were still up," he said in a voice that was studiously casual, "and I thought I'd get a dish of ice cream."

· 7 ·

"On certain mornings, when the atmosphere is truly transparent, I can discern the Ferris wheel, the water chute, the merry-go-round, the whip, the roller coaster, and the whirling airplanes," said Nigel with obvious satisfaction. He was leaning against the wall by the window, his feet crossed at the ankles. In his right hand he held an orange tennis ball, and from time to time he bounced it on the carpeted floor. "Do you suppose they have a sword swallower, Edward? I once knew a shoplifter who had perfected the technique of swallowing diamond rings, so that when he was searched they never caught him with the goods. An Algerian, he was, named Haroun something or other. But Richard would never permit me to go to Holiday Park—not in a million years. Ludwig Wittgenstein, the philosopher, believed that

35

what was imaginable was possible, but Ludwig apparently had never met anyone as pigheaded as my brother. Maybe it's just as well. I probably couldn't stand the noise, anyway. Speaking of noise, did you hear a scream last night?"

Osgood preserved his slightly bored expression. "A scream? From one of the boats out on the water?" he asked. "No, I didn't."

"It was around one o'clock—a sharp, brief, plaintive cry."

"You must've had a nightmare, Nigel."

"Perhaps. I often do." The lunatic grinned artlessly, then scowled, then grinned again. Continuing in a warmer tone, he said, "I've been thinking about your radio, Edward, and have decided you may use it while you're on duty—providing, of course, that I can't hear it."

"Hey, that's great," Osgood responded, although a part of his mind was still engrossed by the scream in the night. "I'll keep it low—and with those Archer earphones of mine, you won't even know it's on."

Nigel bounced the ball and caught it neatly. "My father liked music—loud music—which is why it fills me with abhorrence," he said, turning his head to look out the window at the sea. "At least Scarp Island is a quiet place, I must admit that. Nevertheless, I can't say I'm happy on this damned isolated rock. Even as a boy I hated it here. And I can't stand that treacherous ocean, either—all that deep, deep water between me and freedom. Did you know the word 'isolated' means literally on an island? *Isola* is Italian for island. Interesting, eh? I was furious when they shifted me to this miserable seagull roost from Parkstone Hospital, positively furious."

"You mean you'd rather be in an insane asylum, Nigel?"

"Certainly, Edward. Parkstone wasn't bad, and I'm sure I could have escaped if I'd stayed there another week or so. I was unraveling a broadloom rug in my room, and

36

braiding the pieces of wool together into a very service-
able rope. I had manufactured eight feet of it already. But
they took me away before I could carry out my plan. I
daresay your Uncle Richard tells the world he keeps me
on Scarp for my own good, though it's a damned lie."

Nigel threw the tennis ball down to the floor again,
and snatched it at the top of its ascent. Then he rotated it
slowly in his long fingers, inspecting its orange surface
with narrowed eyes. "Even Montana was better than this,
cold as it got in the wintertime," he said resentfully. "I
was shanghaied out of there by a couple of his
mercenaries—gangsters who drugged me with a doc-
tored cup of cocoa and bundled me off after midnight in a
black limousine. And why were they able to do that?
Because some unprincipled judge in Helena was slipped
a packet of cash to sign his ignoble name on a court order."

"Money works like magic," said Osgood, resting his
elbow on the ledge of the opening. "But wasn't there a
little trouble there in Montana?" he added, with a trace of
a smile. "Before you left, I mean."

"I suppose you're referring to Conrad Schwarzacher,
the Austrian thug I strangled with the suspenders. That
had nothing to do with my being moved. Actually, I was
taken from Glenville because of certain remarks I made to
a visiting reporter for the local paper—remarks about my
brother's political shenanigans. The reporter phoned the
story into a wire service, and the next day it appeared in a
Washington newspaper. Richard, who was a congressman
then, had a fit. He'd been busy delivering windy orations
on the subject of corruption in government all over the
place, and my revelations sawed the limb out from under
him." Nigel glanced toward the window again. "Look!
There's a piping plover," he exclaimed brightly. "What
pretty birds they are! That one's a male. I'd love to catch
him, and keep him on a long, long string."

"This story," Osgood said. "What was it about?"

"Oh, I simply told of how my brother extorted a

hundred thousand dollars from a construction company in Portsmouth, by threatening to condemn eight bridges that were part of Route 40. I had the facts—all the details—and I even offered to sign an affidavit. But somehow Richard managed to avoid being indicted, though it gave him an awful scare. Right after the interview I was smuggled out of Glenville, kept for a while at Parkstone, and eventually brought here in a straightjacket and with a gag in my mouth." A sneer curled the madman's lips, and he bounced the ball so hard on the carpet that it almost rebounded to the ceiling. Grabbing it backhanded as it fell, he concluded bitterly, "And that, Edward, is really how I became the prisoner of Scarp Island."

They were both silent for a while. The chiming of a buoy bell, measured and mournful, suddenly became audible. At last Osgood inquired, "But where did you get the information, Nigel?"

"What information?" the other asked, knitting his brow.

"The information about the extortion—about the hundred thousand dollars."

"Oh. I got it from here, two years earlier. I got it from that trick safe they have up at Grayhaven, the one behind the mantel in the den."

"You mean he kept incriminating evidence in his own house? Wasn't that pretty dumb?"

"I'll say it was. He got away with it, though, didn't he? There's incriminating evidence in that safe right now, I'd be willing to wager—and piles of money, as well. They've been using it for decades, both Richard and my father. Did you ever meet my father, Edward?"

"Once—at Aunt Glenda's funeral."

"He had hairy nostrils—very hairy nostrils. I sometimes wondered how he could breathe. I'm glad I don't have hairy nostrils. Why would so many people vote for a man with such hairy nostrils? I couldn't stand the sight of them. The Portsmouth deal was only one of many that were carefully noted in a small loose-leaf notebook kept by Richard's secretary, that rodent Leon Perth. It covered the transaction from beginning to end, giving the dates the four payments were made and the dates the money was sent to Switzerland by courier. A hundred thousand is a sizable sum, isn't it? Think of all the food it could buy for starving people. They say the population explosion is going to produce famines of incredible dimensions. Millions will perish. How strange it is! The world has an enormous excess of human beings, but if you kill just one of them they treat you like a criminal."

"And this safe is up at Grayhaven, Nigel?" Osgood said, pursuing the part of his companion's conversation that most interested him.

"Yes, in the den. I suppose they felt it was a secure place. On an island you don't have to worry much about burglars, or about the police making sudden swoops, do you?" Nigel squeezed the tennis ball, and the muscles in his forearm stood out like cables. "Then, too, that mantelpiece is cunningly contrived. Unless you know the secret, you'd never be able to pull it out from the wall. It works on bronze ball bearings, and there are springs and counterweights that facilitate its operation. Over the mantel, you see, there's a painting, and the hook that supports it is actually a key. Give it a half-turn and it unlocks the mechanism. Once that's done, all you have to do is fiddle with the ornamental carving on each side of the fireplace and the entire unit swings out on hinges. It's a nifty arrangement, really, because it can't be opened by accident. For years I knew there was a safe behind that mantel, but I could never discover how to get at it, until one afternoon I saw Richard perform the necessary ritual by the merest chance. I happened to be behind the drapes in the bay window—hiding from the world. At that time I was depressed, on the brink of psychosis. I've been thinking, Edward. Would it be possible for you to get me a balloon?"

"A balloon?" the youth repeated, bewildered by the sudden transition.

"Yes—from Holiday Park. An orange one, full of helium so it can soar up into the air. The largest you can find."

"Sure," Osgood answered. "I'll get you one. And they keep valuables in that safe, too?"

"You won't forget, will you?" Nigel asked, his expression an odd blend of delight and anxiety.

"No, no. I'll bring it Tuesday morning."

"Do you promise?"

"I promise. An orange balloon—full of helium."

Nigel beamed at him.

"But you mentioned money in the safe," Osgood said insistently. "Where does the money come from?"

"Graft," the lunatic replied. "I wish I'd known how to open that mantel sooner. I could have really blown the lid off my father's crooked plots and evil machinations. As it was, I did manage to pass on some information to the Providence *Journal*—information I obtained by eavesdropping at home while the old boy was conniving with a group of his henchmen. My contribution played a part in his defeat for a second term in the Senate. They always suspected me of being the source of that leak, but they couldn't prove it. Ha, ha! Not long after that, my father had his first heart attack—in the evening around eight o'clock. He was listening to *Turandot* on his Magnavox, and I was upstairs trying to read an essay by De Quincey, though the walls were vibrating from the sound.

"That attack didn't kill him, but it certainly brought him down a peg. From then on he spent every night in his wing chair in the parlor, swaddled like the Infant Jesus in sheets and blankets. Do you understand why, Edward? It was because the old reprobate was terrified of entering

40

his bed and never leaving it again—of going to sleep on his pillow and never waking up. He thought if he stayed in his chair, Death wouldn't know he was sick. He thought he could outsmart the ravenous reaper, fool the grim ferryman, hornswoggle Atropos the way he had hornswoggled so many trusting mortals. But it didn't work. He died that spring, squirming on the floor like a caterpillar pinned to a shingle. Everyone came to his funeral—even his red-haired mistress from New Haven. There were carloads of flowers and no end of sympathy cards, yet I'm sure I wasn't the only happy person present. Who knows, maybe they were all delighted, eh?"

Nigel stuffed the tennis ball in his pocket, then scratched his thatch of asphalt-colored hair with a finger curved like a claw.

"But . . . but didn't you feel a little bit sorry for your father?" Osgood asked him, incredulous.

"No. Why should I have?" the man answered. "He was a wretch, Edward—a villain. He took money from dope peddlers, pimps, cutthroats. He took money from hotel owners who didn't want to install fire doors, from bankers who sought increased mortgage interest rates, from lawyers for quick paroles, from abortionists, from building contractors who needed lenient inspectors to approve unsafe structures, from loan sharks and racketeers. I think I'll make some fudge. Do you like fudge?"

"Yes . . . sure," said Osgood.

"Good. MacKenzie would never eat my fudge. He didn't trust me. You know, I should have killed MacKenzie when I had him. Then they would have had to send me to an asylum," Nigel declared with a vacant grin. "I myself love fudge. The Mayas used cacao beans for money, they thought so highly of them. A slave could be bought for a hundred beans—roughly the amount required for the brewing of four pots of hot chocolate. Isn't that fascinating? There were even counterfeiters who removed the cocoa from the bean pod and replaced it with sand. Mixed with the genuine article, it passed for the real McCoy. Caveat emptor, eh?"

He walked away from the window and went towards his kitchenette in the alcove.

"Does your brother realize you know how to open that safe, Nigel?" Osgood called after him.

"No, he doesn't. Why?"

"But after the information you gave to the reporter . . ."

"Oh, when Richard asked me about that I told him I got the stuff from a loose-leaf book that I found on a table in the den one summer afternoon. Ha, ha! That way he suspected nothing, and Leon Perth—the damned lackey—had to absorb all the blame." Nigel dumped cocoa into a saucepan. "Are you quite certain you didn't hear a scream last night, Edward?" he inquired in a childish voice.

"I didn't hear a thing," Osgood replied, watching him intently.

"Odd . . . distinctly odd," said the lunatic. "I do hope my auditory hallucinations aren't coming back. That's all I need."

· 8 ·

After they had given Nigel his dinner and dined themselves, they went to the jetty and sat at the very end of it with their legs dangling over the murky green water.

"I don't know why you're still angry," said Osgood.

"Why shouldn't I be?" she answered, clasping her hands tightly together in her lap.

"Because I've apologized a dozen times, that's why."

"A few words—what do they mean?" she asked bitterly. "Do you really think you can . . ."

The girl halted abruptly, blinking her hazel eyes.

"It wasn't my fault, Adriana," he said, frowning. "I didn't mean to hurt you, but . . ."

"But what?"

"I got carried away, and . . . and you were so stubborn."

"Stubborn? I had a right to be, didn't I? It's my body, Edward, and I shouldn't have to do anything with it I don't want to."

"Sure, sure," he conceded hastily. "Cripes, don't get so upset. You'll start crying again."

"No, I won't," she said with dignity. "You needn't worry."

The two of them gazed out at the sea. There was no wind and the water, shimmering beneath the red rays of the setting sun, stretched like a satin sheet to the gray land in the distance. Only the bobbing buoy that marked a submarine crag, its bell tolling softly, broke the flat smooth surface.

"Sex is no big deal, you know, in this day and age," Osgood muttered. "I mean, the average person doesn't consider it a fate worse than death any more."

"That has nothing to do with it," she snapped. "I don't consider it a fate worse than death, either, but I do think I'm entitled to choose my partner. And I'm entitled to tender treatment, too."

"Well, I figured you liked me . . . otherwise I never would have made a pass."

"A pass? A pass? Is that what you call it?" she said sarcastically. "Some people might call it rape, I imagine."

"Oh, Adriana—come on!"

"My legs still hurt . . . and my wrists, too." She held out her hands. "Look at the bruises."

He shook his head and said, "You must bruise easily."

"I do—and not just externally, either."

"God, you talk as though I punched you around," he complained irritably. "I only held you tight, that's all. Making love is a physical thing. It's not like reading a book or watching television."

"True, but it shouldn't be an act of aggression . . . a conflict. It shouldn't be a demonstration of brute force."

In the south, a two-engined patrol plane appeared. It approached them slowly, a toy in the immensity of the darkening sky. Osgood looked up at it, wishing he were the pilot. Then, as it was humming by over their heads, the nurse said to him, "How many women have you treated that way, Edward? Quite a few, I suppose."

He almost smiled. "Most girls aren't so hard to get along with," he answered, sidestepping the question.

"I'm sure they aren't—not with you. They must all find you irresistible. And when you get back to Providence tomorrow, no doubt there'll be hordes of them impatiently awaiting your arrival."

"No, you're wrong. I'm not the sort of dude who bounces from one woman to another, Adriana. I mean, I don't go in for casual sex. If I don't have pretty strong feelings for a girl, I won't touch her. Like with you. I was attracted right away, from the moment I walked into that office—which is why I didn't have much self-control last night. But if I'd known you didn't want me—really didn't want me—then I wouldn't have even tried to kiss you. I honestly thought you liked me."

"I haven't said I don't," she declared. "I only said I don't want to be manhandled—treated as if I wasn't even human. If I didn't have some feeling for you, I would've made a big fuss about it to Mr. Vaughan."

The nurse bowed her head and began to sob. A crystalline tear trickled down her tanned cheek, leaving behind it a thin silvery trail.

"Don't cry," Osgood said, putting his arm around her shoulders. "There's nothing to be sad about, Adriana. I give you my word I'll never be rough with you again—honest. Okay?"

She looked up at him with tearful sparkling eyes, and smiled wanly. He drew her towards him and kissed her lips.

From the barred window of his bedroom, Nigel Vaughan observed them through his little opera glasses, as the sinking sun made streaks of crimson fire of the few lenticular clouds that hovered above the western horizon.

· 9 ·

Early the following morning Edward Osgood left Adriana Danziger's warm, faintly lilac-scented bed, went up to his own room, packed a small valise, and hurried from the cottage. So eager was he to begin his long weekend vacation that he helped Flowers and the handyman Muldoon to unload three drums of diesel fuel for the electric generator, as well as cartons of fresh eggs, milk, butter, meat, frozen vegetables, and other groceries for the denizens of Scarp. Within fifteen minutes of the youth's arrival the *Monica-Mae* had left the jetty and was rumbling across the bay in the direction of Fairoaks pier.

That afternoon Adriana answered the cottage doorbell and found Louise Vaughan pacing the patchy front lawn with quick, nervous steps. She wore an almost-transparent violet T-shirt, no bra, snug mustard-colored shorts, and white, thonged sandals. To the nurse, her slender body appeared as supple as an acrobat's.

Approaching the open door but halting well before the threshold, the visitor asked, "How's your patient? Still as high-spirited as ever?"

"Nigel's fine, Mrs. Vaughan," Adriana answered. "He'll be delighted to see you."

"I'm not going up, dear—not today. Some other time."

"Oh. It won't upset him. On the contrary, it will make him very happy."

"I'm sure you're right, but it might upset me. The poor man reacts so . . . passionately when he sees me. All that gooey chatter, all those protestations of undying devotion—I simply can't bear it. Sentiment isn't my strong suit, I'm afraid. Has he fractured any more arms lately?"

"No, no. His behavior's been perfectly normal," the nurse said. "Actually I think he regrets having hurt Mr. MacKenzie."

"Do you? I doubt it myself. Nigel's remorseless. His view of life is so topsy-turvy that broken arms don't count for much. His concept of good and bad, of morality, is completely screwed up. He once told me that if he were forced to make a choice between lying under oath and committing a murder, he'd commit the murder without a moment's hesitation. And that was years ago, when he was still fairly rational. For him, physical violence is trivial compared to loyalty, justice, and so on. How's the new boy?"

"Edward? He's working out very well. Nigel seems to like him. I thought he'd have trouble adjusting to a stranger, but I was wrong. Edward will be better company for him than Mr. MacKenzie was."

"And for you, too, I should think," said Louise in a voice with no inflection. "I'll tell Richard. He'll be pleased. The great man likes things to go smoothly. I met Edward on the beach a couple of days ago. Handsome creature, isn't he?"

"Yes," Adriana replied, feeling the blood mount to her cheeks. "Handsomer than Mr. MacKenzie, at any rate."

Mrs. Vaughan smiled thinly. "If I'm any judge, he's one of those carefree lusty lads—quick off the mark, as they say. Better keep your door bolted at night, Adriana."

"He impressed me as more serious than that," the girl answered, her face a terra-cotta pink. "Yesterday, he and Nigel had a long conversation about Greek philosophy. Edward was interested in Plato, and Nigel treated him to an hour's lecture."

"It must have been exciting. Has he gone away for the weekend?"

46

"He left this morning. Did you want to speak to him, Mrs. Vaughan?"

"Not particularly, dear. I'm just out for a little promenade. Richard and Leon are entertaining a disgusting old ruffian up at the house—a political power from some hick town. At lunch the son-of-a-bitch kept putting his fat greasy hand on my leg under the table. If I hadn't been afraid of making Richard peevish, I would've ladled a few ounces of iced vichyssoise into the bastard's lap. That would have cooled his ardor. Give Nigel my love, will you?"

"Of course. You're sure you don't want to see him?" Adriana asked hopefully.

"Yes, I'm sure," the woman retorted firmly. "Goodbye, dear."

· 10 ·

An unseasonal blast of cold Canadian air had swept into the region during the night, and the island was shrouded in a dense, restless, dove-gray mist. From the gently rocking motor launch, Osgood could only just discern the floodlights on the dock and some random discs of saffron illumination, faint and fuzzy, at what he knew to be the top of the hill. It was a desolate scene.

Once ashore, he went directly to his room, ate a breakfast of ham and eggs, and took a hot shower. Having drunk too much and slept too little the previous three days, his mind was dull and his mood less than cheerful. While he was dressing he spied Adriana walking through the fog towards the mainhouse. He threw up his window and called to her, but his voice didn't carry in the humid air and she failed to hear him.

Around ten o'clock he arrived in the corridor, lit a cigarette, sat back in the chair, and glowered up at the ceiling.

Immediately Nigel's V-shaped countenance appeared at the barred aperture. "Where is it, Edward?" he asked.

"Where is what?" Osgood responded gruffly.

"The balloon, of course—my orange balloon."

"Oh, that," said the youth, putting his feet on the desk. "I didn't get it. I'll get it the next time."

A look of disbelief spread over Nigel's face. "You didn't get it?" he said in a cracked voice.

"I couldn't. The park wasn't open. It doesn't open until noontime."

"But . . . but you could have bought it the night before."

"The night before, Nigel, I was in Providence."

"What's that got to do with it?" the prisoner asked. "Did you or did you not promise to bring me an orange balloon, Edward?"

"I'll pick it up next time."

"Next time is fourteen days away, damn it. You should have inconvenienced yourself a little to fulfill your promise. A pledge is a pledge. You could have come back last night. What difference does it make whether you sleep here or there?"

"To me, a big difference," Osgood replied nastily, the cigarette hanging from the side of his mouth.

For a full minute Nigel glared at him with eyes that were like nodules of blue ice. Then he said, "I see," and retreated into his living room.

His attendant muttered a curse, slumped further down into the swivel chair, closed his eyes, and puffed spasmodically on the cigarette. Out on the ocean a foghorn hooted. When its plaintive squawk came to an end, the rhythmic thumping of Nigel's footsteps—like the pounding of a palpitating heart—could be heard on the carpeted floor.

Osgood opened the desk drawer that contained his portable radio, donned the headset, and switched the instrument on. Muted strains of West Coast jazz seeped into his ears and beguiled his weary brain. He wondered if Adriana would fill in for him for a couple of hours, so he could take a nap. The men on the launch had told him "the gentry" had left the island Sunday night. With his uncle gone, he reflected, there was no reason for him to be stuck in the corridor all day.

While he was busy with these thoughts, something struck him on the top of the head, almost knocking him out of the chair. A geyser of colored light erupted inside his cranium. Yanking off the earphones, he groggily got to his feet and looked around wildly. Nigel was at the door again, his arm protruding from the opening. In his hand he held a long tube of newspaper. It was slightly tapered and more than an inch wide at its narrowest end.

"You hit me," Osgood said stupidly.

"Yes," Nigel admitted.

"With that."

"Of course. Hard, isn't it? I manufacture these things out of my morning *Times*, gluing the sheets together with syrup or jam or gravy. Works surprisingly well."

"You might have fractured my skull."

"I doubt it. To do that I'd need at least a sledgehammer."

Osgood made a lunge for the tube, twisted it out of the madman's hand, and smashed it down on the edge of the desk. It bent but didn't break. Several more whacks were necessary before the tough papier mâché cylinder was reduced to pieces small enough to drop in the wastebasket.

"If you try anything like that again, Nigel, I'll go back to my room and leave you here alone," said the youth, retrieving his smoldering cigarette from under the chair and snuffing it out in the ashtray.

"Ho, ho!" Nigel exclaimed derisively. "You'll run off and sulk, will you? Might as well, you're not much company anyway. Did you have a big weekend, boy? Paint the town vermilion? You look positively cadaverous, and your eyes are like stained-glass windows. I figured you for a voluptuary the minute I saw you. You're a gin-hound and a carouser, eh? That's why you forgot my balloon, isn't it? Your wretched brain was too soaked in alcohol to function properly. What can honor and loyalty mean to a damned swillbelly like you?"

Before Osgood had a chance to reply, Nigel vanished once again, and the thumping footfalls recommenced.

For the better part of an hour, all was peaceful. The attendant, earphones clamped back on his head, sat dozing in his chair. His breathing was deep and regular, his arms and legs as limp as wet clay. Perspiration formed a film on his forehead, and occasionally his lowered eyelids would flicker like a baby's. Then the acrid smell of smoke trickled into the young man's nostrils, causing him to awaken abruptly. He saw at once that there were little jets of white vapor coming from under the golden oak door of the living room.

"Fire!" he gasped, ripping off the headset and jumping from the chair. An ominous crackling noise sent chills down his spine. "Nigel!" he called, crossing the corridor. "Are you all right?"

Because of the fog and the fact that no lamps were lit, the interior of the apartment was dim as a cave. He peered through the opening, through a veil of smoke at the vague shadows beyond. Suddenly a long-fingered hand shot out of the gloom, snaked between the steel bars, and grabbed him by the hair. An instant later Nigel's grinning visage rose up from below, disembodied by the fumes and the darkness.

"Caught you fair and square," he growled triumphantly. "First try, too. How could a clever lad like you, Edward, be taken in by such a simple ruse? A bit of burning wash cloth and the crumpling of a page from the *Times*—that was all I needed. A hoary, ancient dodge. But perhaps you're not really clever. Perhaps you're a trifle slow-witted—a boob, a ninny, a simp, a dunce."

50

"Let go," said Osgood, doing his best to stay calm while he tried with both hands to loosen the iron grip which clutched the thickest part of his shaggy mane. "Let go. If you don't, Nigel, I'll call Adriana."

"Call all you like. Bellow at the top of your lungs—please do. But unless your voice is a good deal more powerful than your intelligence, Edward, I'm afraid she won't hear you. Miss Danziger is at Grayhaven, in the library. This morning I had a sudden craving for Mr. Hardy of Wessex. Forlorn captives like me can only travel spiritually. If I wish to visit a quaint village or a sylvan setting, if I wish to meet picturesque characters and hear pithy conversations, I can do so by means of books alone. They're my one form of transportation. Isn't that sad, Edward?"

"If you don't let me go immediately," Osgood said, "I'll have to report this to your brother."

By now his head was twisted around to such a degree that he could see his tormentor only from the corners of his eyes.

"Suit yourself," Nigel answered placidly. "Do you like Hardy? For me he's a perennial. Ha, ha! Don't struggle so, my boy, you'll strain something."

"I'll tell Uncle Richard. I swear I will."

"Nonsense. Don't you know that in the whole of nature there is nothing as vacuous as an empty threat? You'll tell Uncle Richard. Ha! He may learn of this eventually, Edward, but not from your perfidious lips—unless some spiritualist can raise you at a seance."

To emphasize this last sally, the madman gave the youth's head a playful rap with his knuckles, and then chuckled fiendishly.

"Ouch!" Osgood cried. "That hurt. What are you going to do? I thought we were friends, Nigel. What are you going to do?"

"Can't you guess, boy? Why, I'm going to bring you in here to join me, that's what I'm going to do. Won't that be nice? Of course your body may not fit, being a bit bulky, but your head should come through all right."

"No . . . no! It won't. It can't. The bars are too close together," Osgood protested, a distinct note of dread in his voice.

"Rubbish," said the lunatic, beginning to tug in earnest. "The space is more than adequate—five or six inches, I'd estimate. If anything, it's your head that's the wrong size. It's altogether too swollen, too fat. And your skull is too damned thick, into the bargain. Still, since it doesn't house anything—no brain to speak of—it ought to compress fairly easily. All that's required is a certain amount of strenuous pulling and hauling on my part, and a modicum of patience and fortitude on yours. 'Never complain, never explain,' Disraeli used to say. Once we're past the lumpy part, it should glide through like a thing on wires."

"No—you're hurting me, Nigel. It won't fit, I tell you."

"Of course it won't. Not if you're going to wriggle about that way. Please exhibit some manliness, otherwise it will be quite impossible for me to do the job neatly."

By this time the unyielding bars were pinching Osgood's crown like the jaws of a vise. "Stop!" he bawled frantically. "Stop, for chrissake. I never harmed you."

"You never brought me my balloon, either. Vengeance, I've always thought, is one of the virtues. If not, why do we enjoy tragedy? Why does it purge us, eh? You forgot my balloon, Edward, so I've decided to use your head for a balloon. It isn't orange but one can't have everything, can one? After I wrench it off, clean it up a little and run a string through the nostrils, it should serve my purpose splendidly. I daresay it will float like a dirigible, too, being inflated with false promises and other types of hot air. Come along, now. Don't be intransigent, boy."

With each of the many taut filaments in Nigel's straining hand making its poignant contribution, the pain in Osgood's scalp was scarcely bearable. It was as if his flesh and hair were slowly, inexorably, being torn away. Yet agonizing as this torture was, the terrible pressure on the skull itself constituted an infinitely worse discomfort. And, since he could no longer see the barred opening, he was able to imagine that half his head had already been squeezed into the narrow gap, and that he could actually hear the splintering of bone and feel his brain disintegrating.

Desperate, he tried again to unlock the madman's iron grip, and simultaneously kicked out with his legs and shouted as loud as he could. By chance, his foot came in contact with the open desk drawer, dislodged it, and sent it flying down the corridor. The small radio tumbled out onto the carpet, and the place was suddenly resounding to the vibrant harmonies of a lively Dixieland band.

At once Nigel began yelling in his ear, but because of the music and his own distress, Osgood couldn't grasp what he was saying. It was a moment, therefore, before the young man realized that the lunatic was pleading with him to put an end to the noise.

"Turn it off. Turn it off. Turn it off," he kept repeating. "Turn it off, please."

"If you don't let me go, how can I?" the attendant cried.

Instantly his head was released. Weak from fear and exertion, he slid down the oak door to his knees.

"Turn it off, Edward!" Nigel implored, from further back in his apartment. "Please turn off the radio."

On all fours Osgood crawled to the transistor and poked the button that halted its boisterous transmission. Stillness returned to the hall with a jolting abruptness. The convulsive rasp of his own breathing was now all that could be heard. Osgood felt the top of his head with trembling fingers, and found to his surprise that he wasn't bleeding, though the grinding, stinging pain in his skull and scalp had abated only a little.

Regaining some of his composure, he retrieved the
radio, earphones, and drawer, and put them back where
they belonged. This done, he went on shaky legs into the
pantry, and from there on to his room. A few minutes later
he returned, carrying a small object in his right hand.

"Nigel!" he called hoarsely. "Nigel, you goddamned
nut case, don't ever try anything like that again. You hear
me? Because if you do, Nigel, I'm going to cut your goddamned arm off at the elbow—with this."

Osgood raised his hand aloft. There was a sharp click,
and a shiny blade of steel, long and pointed, whipped out
from the object he was holding.

At that moment Adriana entered the corridor, but the
youth, in the throes of his anger, scarcely noticed her.

"There's seven inches of it, Nigel, and it's sharp as a
razor," he yelled, waving the antler-handled knife wildly
in front of the barred opening. "And from now on I'm
carrying it with me at all times."

If the man inside the darkened room heard these
threats, however, he gave no indication of it. The only
sound that broke the silence was another hoot from the
foghorn out at sea.

· 11 ·

"Who's calling?" the woman asked in a businesslike
tone.

"Edward Osgood," he answered, recognizing the
voice immediately.

"Oh, Edward . . . Edward of the beach," she said, her
manner suddenly familiar. "Did you have a pleasant
swim that night, Edward?"

"Yes, Mrs. Vaughan. It was fine."

"Not too cold or choppy for you?"

"No, it was perfect."

"Good. Swimming is such a wholesome form of exercise. It'll keep your muscles nice and firm, dear. How are Nigel and Adriana?"

"Okay," he replied laconically. In the background he could hear the garbled speech of two men—one with a high voice, one with a low. "Is Mr. Vaughan busy?"

"Not too busy for you, Edward," she declared, mildly mocking him. "Hold on."

Two or three minutes passed before the politician finally got on the line. "Yes, Edward," he said querulously. "Anything wrong?"

Osgood apologized for bothering him and then rapidly related the story of Nigel's vicious assault, presenting the tale as vividly as he was able.

"Are you injured?" Vaughan inquired, when he had finished.

"Well, I've had a stiff neck and a bad headache all day," he answered, "but my skull is still in one piece, as far as I can tell."

"I see. A pity you let him trick you that way."

"What could I do, Uncle Richard? I thought the place was on fire."

"Yes . . . yes. He's clever—very clever. You haven't lost your nerve, though, have you? I hope you're not going to let him frighten you off, Edward."

"Me? No. I don't scare that easy," Osgood said with casual assurance. "But he's a rough customer. I didn't know when I took the job about some of those violent things he did . . . the things he did before he came here, I mean."

"Come now. You were fully warned," the politician said reprovingly. "How many times did I caution you? How many times did I stress the importance, the absolute necessity, of staying out of Nigel's reach?" The vigorous baritone voice softened slightly. "But it must have been a shocking experience for you. It was a great stroke of luck, the radio going on that way. Isn't it odd how noise affects him? The doctors say it's a conditioned reflex. My father played the radio loudly, because he was a bit hard of hearing. And in Nigel's turbulent brain, noise has been associated with paternal discipline ever since. The old man used to thrash him on occasions."

"I hope I don't have to take the radio out of there, Uncle Richard. That wouldn't be fair, would it? I didn't start the trouble—he did. And it's awfully boring sitting at that desk all day long with nothing to pass the time."

"Do the headphones still work?"

"Yes, they're as good as ever."

"Very well, then keep your radio there. I doubt if he'll raise a fuss—and, under the circumstances, you deserve a few amenities. I'll have a word with Perth, too, so that your next paycheck will carry an increase."

"Thanks. I appreciate that," said Osgood, delighted.

"You're entirely welcome. Of course, you won't talk about this unfortunate incident to anyone, will you? We can't afford to be indiscreet about what occurs on the island. Gossip can create fearful problems for a man in public life, Edward."

"Oh, don't worry. I won't say a word, Uncle Richard. I know how to keep things to myself."

"Excellent. I'm glad you called," Vaughan said. "I like to be kept informed. Watch yourself in the future. Good-bye."

· 12 ·

After the incident, Nigel was sullen and hostile for several days. Nor was Edward much better. He hardly spoke to the prisoner and, when he did, his remarks were far from gracious. But it was Adriana who bore the brunt of the quarrel, since she was obliged to listen to the complaints of both parties. Offering sympathy to each of the men in turn, she gradually soothed their ruffled feelings, and by Friday things were virtually back to normal again.

56

The nurse left Scarp that afternoon and went to Cambridge, Massachusetts, to spend the weekend with her married sister. For the three days she was gone and though Osgood was on his own, no problems arose. Every night the girl phoned him, and their conversations were long and intimate. When she returned Monday evening, she was so loaded down with colorful shopping bags that Henry Coombs, the boatman, had to carry her suitcase to the cottage. For 'Ned,' as she had begun to call Osgood, she had bought two fancy sport shirts and an expensive traveling alarm clock, while for Nigel she had obtained six books and three bars of Swiss chocolate. But most of the bags held blouses, skirts, shorts, jeans, and dresses for herself.

During the period that followed—it was towards the end of June—the weather became tropically warm. From dawn to dusk the yellow sun beamed mercilessly out of a sky as transparent as flint glass. No breath of wind stirred the torrid air, no drop of rain moistened the sandy soil. The wild red roses withered on their spiked branches. The lawns were left with brittle shards of brown grass that snapped and crepitated beneath a walker's feet; any strolls along the narrow trails that intersected the slopes of the hill were sure to generate roiling clouds of dust and grit. The island took on the appearance of a desert.

On these scorching days, Edward Osgood and Adriana Danziger ate their lunches together at a secluded stretch of beach facing the blue, seemingly limitless Atlantic Ocean. Here the waves, having discovered a vulnerable point in the stony shoreline, had gnawed from it a small crescent cove. This miniature harbor, surrounded as it was by bluffs crowned with heather and blackberry bushes, and lined from one cusp to the other with fine golden sand, provided them with a retreat that was as private as it was comfortable, and as charming as it was romantic.

Day after day they lolled and dallied there, exchanging ardent vows and amorous favors. Day after day they laughed and frolicked, while the rays of the sun simmered their young bodies to a coppery bronze. And day by day their lives grew evermore entangled.

· 13 ·

"Faced with prolonged misery and certain death, the so-called normal man has desperate need of tricks and stratagems if he wishes to go on living," said Nigel, as he cut his fingernails with a clipper. "Confronted with the stark horror of reality, the sane person requires all manner of illusions—defense mechanisms, they're aptly termed—in order to survive, for without these self-deceptions he would have motivation for nothing but suicide."

"A pretty gloomy idea," Osgood commented indifferently.

"I'll say it is—yet true nonetheless. I helped a man commit suicide at Rose Hill Manor, years ago. Showed him how to tear his shirt-sleeves off and twist them into a noose. There was a great furor when they found him hanging from a pipe in the bathroom. They cut him down in such haste that his body landed on the washbasin and tore it off the wall. There was water everywhere. A Frenchman once killed himself with a grand piano. He hoisted it up to the ceiling with ropes and pulleys, made himself comfortable underneath it, and then cut the thing loose. It must have flattened him into a crepe suzette, eh? A bizarre race, the French. Gerard de Nerval, a fine poet, used to drink his wine from a human skull. He claimed it was his mother's, and that he had to kill her to get it. Ha, ha! What I'm saying, Edward, is that normal people aren't as sure sighted as they believe—that the images registering on their brains are not the same as those their eyes beheld initially. As Edgar Allen Poe observed,

'All that we see or seem,

Is but a dream within a dream.'
So when psychiatrists contend that madmen lose touch
with reality, the good doctors are deluding themselves.
It's the sane who dwell in a fantasy world, and the insane
who see things as they actually are. That's why they go
crazy."

Nigel carefully clipped the nail on his thumb, cutting
it almost to the quick.

Osgood said, "I've been wondering about that safe
up at Grayhaven—wondering why your brother would
keep large amounts of money there."

"Where else should he keep it?"

"Well . . . in a bank, like other people."

"But he can't do that, you see," Nigel said, grinning
elfishly. "The income-tax bloodhounds check up on all
sizable bank deposits. They want their share." He blew a
piece of nail out of the jaws of the clipper. "And even if he
were willing to pay the tax, there would be other government agents who'd be curious to know where the money
came from in the first place. Crooks have their problems,
too."

"So he keeps it here until he can have some guy
sneak it out of the country to Switzerland," said Osgood
meditatively.

"Exactly. Then, when he needs a lot of capital to
finance an election or some other big operation, he gets
the money back by devious means through slick inter-
mediaries in the financial world." Nigel began trimming
his cuticles. "I've been mulling over that safe, also," he
declared. "There could be a small fortune in it—seventy
or eighty thousand dollars. I've seen times when it held as
much as a quarter of a million—enough cash to burn a wet
mule. Ha, ha! Suppose you and I were to steal that money,
Edward, and flee to the mainland, eh? We could do it
some weekend, when there was no one here except the
dotty old Muldoons. The hue and cry wouldn't be raised
for a couple of days, and by then we could be in Bisbee,

Arizona or Godfrey, Illinois. How's that for a nifty idea? You can have the money. I don't want it. Just getting away from this damned Tartarus would be reward enough for me."

Osgood smiled mischievously. "But they'd catch us, Nigel," he pointed out, "and then we'd both be behind bars. And prison is one place I don't want to end up in."

"They wouldn't catch us. How could they? We'd have a terrific headstart. Still, if you're worried about being arrested for theft, there's a method of getting around that. Only take a small portion of the money—two or three thousand—and the chances are they'll never miss it. I often took little sums like that—just to go out and have a good time, you understand—and neither my father or Richard seemed to notice. If they did, they kept silent. After all, whom could they report the loss to? They were criminals themselves. Whom could they complain to? The money's illegal. They daren't go to the police about it." Throwing one of his legs over the arm of the chair, the lunatic inspected his manicure job with grave eyes. "Imagine being crushed by a piano," he said after a while. "The noise must be excruciating."

"No, I don't think I'll do it, Nigel," Osgood said, still smiling. "Too risky. Besides, it's dishonest, isn't it?"

"Nonsense. Stealing from a crook isn't dishonesty. It's retribution. But I knew you wouldn't have the guts. Sane people are afraid of everything. They're not accustomed to harsh reality. 'Delusion is better than the truth sometimes, and fine dreams than dismal waking.' Thackeray said that. He was eminently sane. William Makepeace Thackeray. Beautiful name, isn't it? Lewis Carroll's middle name was Lutwidge. I don't much care for that. Part of the money I took from the safe I spent on my coin collection. I used to have a great quantity of silver dollars. Uncirculated, they were—except for a few."

Nigel folded the clippers, set them on the lucite table, got up and went to the window. "If I had a balloon," he muttered wistfully, "this would be a perfect day to fly it."

· 14 ·

Shortly after the Fourth of July, Richard Vaughan, Louise Vaughan, Leon Perth, and six guests—three middle-aged men and three youngish women—came to Scarp Island, and all the lights at Grayhaven were ablaze. During the evening the sound of laughter and music was often so loud it could be heard at the cottage, causing Nigel to slam his windows shut and complain bitterly.

Around nine-thirty, Osgood and Adriana—who had skipped her weekend ashore to be with her young man—walked up the hill and sat on a small knoll that skirted the mansion's front lawn, in order to watch the convivial group eat its sumptuous dinner in the ornate dining room with the crystal chandeliers. The women were dressed in bright gowns of pastel hues, while the men wore white jackets and dark bow ties. The table's center was crowded with covered bowls, platters, tureens, and wine bottles—and, judging from the flashing of knives, forks, and glassware, all those present were both hungry and thirsty. Mrs. Muldoon, in a little cap and laced apron, flitted about the room like a mechanical doll, entering with full dishes and departing with empty ones.

"Do you suppose we'll ever be rich, Ned?" Adriana asked, resting her head on his shoulder.

"Sure, why not?" he answered. "It isn't hard to become a success in this world—not if you use your brains. Of course, you have to be willing to take a chance now and then, too."

"If we were rich, we'd have everything," she said dreamily. "Wouldn't we?"

"I guess. Look. There's our creepy pal, Leon, tapping another jug of champagne. What a deal he's got! Even so, I wouldn't trade places with him. The guy's a whimp, a zilch—strictly nothing. To be somebody you have to look like somebody. Perth looks like a kid with pernicious anemia."

The nurse giggled. "Pernicious anemia, Ned? Have you been reading my medical books? Maybe I'll make a doctor of you. All right?" she asked, slipping her hand under his loose sweatshirt to pinch his stomach. Then, more seriously, she added, "You have to own your own business to make money, I guess. My sister's brother-in-law opened a small camera shop in Newton three years ago, and now he drives a new Continental."

"I could do something like that, too," Osgood said, his eyes fixed on the distant figure of Louise Vaughan, who was standing up at the table with her stemmed glass held high, evidently proposing a toast. "I know more about stereo equipment than most of those guys selling the stuff. But to get started you need capital."

"I've got that money in the bank, Ned."

"How much does it amount to?"

"Almost twenty-seven hundred."

"It would take a lot more than that, Adriana. Pretty soon I'm going to open an account, too, though. With both of us saving, maybe we could get enough together to make some serious plans. I don't want to spend the rest of my life listening to Nigel's babbling—and I don't want you to, either."

The nurse snuggled up to him and rubbed her face in his hair. "Why don't we go to the cove for a little while? Splash around in the water for an hour or so," she suggested.

"No bathing suits," he answered, grinning.

"Do we need them?" she asked, poking him with a finger beneath the sweatshirt.

"Suppose somebody wanders down there and catches us?"

"Who? Those people? They'll be feasting until ten-thirty or eleven. And after that they'll all troop into the

62

parlor and have coffee and brandy. Come on, Neddy—
let's go."

She jumped up and dragged him to his feet.

It was close to midnight by the time they returned to
the cottage. No sooner had they stepped in the door than
Adriana said, "I forgot my wristwatch. I left it there on the
beach—on the rock. We'll have to go back."

"Cripes," said Osgood, shaking his head in annoyance. "I'll get it. You stay here. I just hope it isn't
under water. The tide was coming in."

He left her and trotted up the hill, taking the most
direct route to the beach on the opposite side of the
island. It was very dark, but the pale gravel of the path was
easily visible against the background of gray green
shrubbery. Reaching the cove in a few minutes, he found
the watch on the flat stone they used as a table for their
picnics. He put it in his pocket and started back.

As he was passing the eastern wing of Grayhaven, a
light flashed on in the den, attracting the youth's attention. Through the large bay windows he saw two of the
male guests, accompanied by Richard Vaughan and Leon
Perth, enter the room. Instinctively, Osgood crouched
down behind a ragged row of stunted pines. Both the
strangers were stout and red-faced. The smaller of the pair
had a trim black chevron-shaped moustache; the larger
was bald except for some tufts of gray hair over his ears,
and had the sleepy eyes of a reptile.

Vaughan offered them cigars from a humidor, which
he then lit with his silver lighter. Meanwhile the diminu-
tive Perth filled brandy snifters from a square decanter
and, when he had served them to the company, discreetly
took a seat in the background.

Mesmerized by the bright tableau framed in the
broad windows no more than thirty feet away, Osgood
stretched out on his stomach on the ground. He was certain he had seen the man with the chevron moustache on

television, and that he was the mayor of one of the larger Providence suburbs.

Big as the room was, it soon clouded with smoke, and the rosy-faced occupants took on a vague resemblance to devils in a steaming netherworld. Richard Vaughan, seated behind a vast mahogany desk, did most of the talking, though the others—except for Perth—made contributions from time to time. What were they gabbing about? Osgood wondered. He could hear their laughter well enough, but the sound of their voices rarely rose above a muted drone.

Sandflies began nibbling on his neck, wrists, and ankles, yet he remained where he was with his eyes glued on the amicable scene. He was surprised to see how subdued Leon Perth was. The usually loquacious secretary had little to say, though he was always quick to join in the general laughter of the others. And if he spied an empty snifter he would hop from his chair, dash for the decanter, and provide a speedy refill with all the finesse of a headwaiter at a fancy restaurant.

"Flunky!" the observer in the shadows muttered contemptuously.

After some twenty minutes of this animated conferring, Richard Vaughan, the cigar jutting from a corner of his mouth, pushed his chair back and stood up. Drawing a brown envelope from inside his beautifully tailored jacket, he came around the desk and passed it to the bald-headed man with the reptilian eyes, who promptly tucked it away in his own coat pocket. Glasses were drained and the others got to their feet. Perth scurried across the room—like a white rat, Osgood thought—to throw open the double doors, while his employer delivered a few more sociable remarks, smiling and gesticulating with the cigar. Then the entire assembly wandered out into the hazy gloom of the hall beyond.

Osgood rolled on his back, sat up, stretched his cramped legs, scratched his neck and ankles, and yawned. A light breeze, tangy with the smell of the sea, stirred the pines and the parched grass of the lawn.

"A political deal, sure as hell," he said softly. "Nigel knows what he's talking about, nutty as he is. There was money in that envelope, I'll bet—a kickback or something."

He stared at the window again. There was the fireplace, behind which a secret safe lay—if the lunatic was to be believed. As he was considering this information, the redheaded Perth reentered the den. Under his arm he carried a small parcel. Almost as if he were influenced in an occult way by Osgood's speculations, the secretary halted before the fireplace, deposited the package on the mantel, and reached up to remove from the wall directly above it a fair-sized gilt-framed picture of what appeared to be a broad, sailboat-covered lake and a range of mountains.

At once the youth's heartbeat began to accelerate. He ducked back behind the evergreens and gazed into the den with reinforced intensity.

After resting the painting on the floor beside a wing chair, Perth dragged a leather hassock to the hearthstone, climbed up on it, and gave the picture hook a quick, dexterous twist. Descending, he then did something to the decorative carvings on each side of the fireplace, and suddenly the whole mantelpiece swung away from the wall like a closet door, revealing the naked brickwork behind it. In this masonry there was a dark gray panel some eighteen inches square, and Perth, moving with an assurance that could only have come from long familiarity, opened this panel and shoved the small parcel into the compartment that lay beyond.

Edward Osgood sighed deeply, and leaned further forward into the stunted pines so as not to miss a thing.

With robotlike efficiency, the secretary shut the little panel, pushed the mantelpiece back against the wall, manipulated the two wood carvings, turned the hook to its original position, and rehung the picture. Once these tasks were finished, he removed the hassock from the hearthstone, picked up the four empty brandy snifters, and departed, switching off the lighted chandelier as he walked out the door.

Osgood waited two or three minutes before getting to his feet. As he walked down the crooked path to the cottage, his black eyes glittered in the darkness as though illuminated from within.

· 15 ·

Two days later in the early afternoon, the six guests, looking wan and weary despite their suntans, boarded the launch and returned to the mainland. From the jetty, Richard Vaughan and Leon Perth waved good-bye to them, treating the visitors with marked deference up to the last moment. Nigel, who watched the proceedings through his binoculars from his living room window, described the scene to Adriana in comical derogatory language that brought frequent smiles to her lips. Osgood wasn't there. Much against his own inclination he had been ordered to help Muldoon replace some broken panes of glass in the greenhouse, and so he spent most of that afternoon mixing putty and listening to the deaf old Irishman's dull stories of his early life in Tullamore.

Throughout that day the sun glared down on the small island, roasting rocks, buildings, people, soil, and vegetation with a supreme impartiality. But towards nightfall, the weather began to change. Banks of gray black clouds appeared on the northern horizon and in a very little time spread over the whole of the twilit sky. Sudden gusts of wind, surprisingly cool for that season of the year, assailed the sparse shrubbery and the gnarled trees, and on the beaches whipped the sand into spiral plumes that looked like columns of beige smoke. Out at sea, sloops, catamarans, yachts, and ketches moved in a steady procession towards Fairoaks harbor, while around them the gray water undulated with a sinister lethargy, like molten lead.

Secure in their cottage, Adriana and Osgood drank a bottle of Lambrusco wine with their dinner that evening, and went to bed together early—though it was some while before they actually felt the need to sleep.

The wind continued to rise, and the temperature to fall. Around midnight, Osgood, shivering from the cold, got up to get another blanket. Then, when he returned to bed, the persistent rattling of one of the windows prevented him from dozing off again. Uttering a soft imprecation, he left Adriana's side a second time, shuffled to the window, lifted the shade, and wedged a book of matches between the sash and the frame. The rattle ceased. As the young man was about to draw the shade down he glimpsed the shadowy mass of Grayhaven at the crown of the hill, and his hand paused in midair. The house was dark from top to bottom, and from one end to the other. All around its spectral form the pines and bushes writhed in the wind.

"If you only took a thousand, nobody would ever miss it," a reasonable voice declared inside his head.

He exhaled his breath, clouding the windowpane, and whispered, "Perth keeps records in a notebook."

"So what?" said the voice. "He could make a mistake. Nigel's already done it several times, and got away with it. But even if they did miss it, how would they know where it went? One of the guests might have taken it, or the Muldoons—or Leon Perth himself. They're not going to suspect you. You've only been here a short while, and you don't live in the mainhouse."

"Nigel could tell them that he spoke to me about the safe, couldn't he? Then where would I be?"

"What if he does? It'll be his word against yours, and he's crazy."

Osgood passed his raised hand across his forehead

and scowled at the distant mansion as though it were the cause of his dilemma. "Suppose I get caught?" he argued silently.

"Who's going to catch you?" the voice asked disdainfully. "They're all asleep, and it's blowing a gale outside."

"But wouldn't it be smarter to wait until they went back to Providence? Wouldn't it be a lot less risky?"

"Sure, but then there'd be fewer suspects, right?" the voice said. "And there's always the possibility that they'll take that little package with them when they go—in which case your quick thousand will be just another busted dream."

Osgood lowered the shade slowly like a man in a daze, but when the action was completed his manner became more decisive. He spun around, snatched his jeans from a chair, and pulled them on. Adriana mumbled in her sleep and nestled further down into the bed. The youth grabbed his sneakers and a heavy sweater, quietly crossed the room, opened the door, and slipped out.

A fine rain was falling. The chill wind drove the drops obliquely over the island's uneven terrain so that Osgood had to face sideways to avoid its stinging onslaught. Up the familiar path he trudged, picking his way by the glow of the floodlight that loomed above the generator hut a hundred yards to his left. In no time at all he found himself standing on the edge of the lawn. Somewhere on the second story an unlatched shutter was banging loudly. It might have been the frantic pounding of a fugitive on a bolted door.

Unwilling to pause for a moment because it would give him the leisure to become afraid, he veered to the right and trotted parallel to the facade of the building until he reached the den's curved windows. A lull in the wind allowed him to hear the angry roar of the sea down at the shore, and the grinding rumble of the agitated shingle. Encouraged by the noise, he raised one of the

68

narrower sashes, pushed back the billowing drapery, and climbed over the sill. The pungent stench of stale cigar smoke greeted him. He shut the window. Above the door to the hall there was a transom, and through it a pearly light filtered, enabling him to see the desk and the other pieces of furniture. Except for the patter of rain and the bluster of the wind, all was comfortingly still.

He strode boldly across the shadowy chamber to the fireplace, took the picture from the wall, and set it down against an end table. As he was so much taller than Perth, he had no need of the hassock to reach the metal hook. Looping his index finger through it, he turned it clockwise as far as it would go. A dull grating sound broke the silence. He now examined the half-pillars that formed the sides of the hearth, and the carvings of oak leaves and acorns that adorned them. A minute of trial-and-error jiggling revealed that both decorations could be slid upward a full two inches, and when he had moved them accordingly the mantelpiece swung away from the wall without a murmur.

"Beautiful," Osgood said in an undertone, and stepped around it.

The next moment, however, his hopes plummeted. In the gray steel panel affixed to the brickwork beside the chimney there was a keyhole. Groaning, he ran his fingers over the little door's border, wondering if it would be possible to pick the lock. The metal rattled loosely. He hooked his thumbnail under its edge and gave a gentle tug. Before his delighted eyes, the panel flew open. Perth, evidently, had placed his faith wholly in the trick mantel, and hadn't bothered to use his key. Perhaps he had stopped using it years ago.

Even as these notions sped through Edward Osgood's mind, his eager hands were busy exploring the safe's interior. The package was there, as well as several notebooks and a velvet-lined box of gold coins. There was a sheaf of papers, most of them correspondence from

Zurich, Nassau, and Panama. There were a half-dozen bulging envelopes; a pile of checkbooks and passbooks, all under strange names; and a cloth bag containing a number of small keys that Osgood shrewdly surmised belonged to safe-deposit boxes somewhere in the world.

Excited by his discoveries, he didn't know what to examine first, but chance made the decision for him. One of the fatter envelopes, jostled from its position on a narrow shelf, fell out of the cubbyhole onto the floor. When he picked it up, the flap opened to reveal a tight stack of new hundred-dollar bills. He caught his breath and leaned against the wall. He had never in his entire life held so much money in his hands. Riffling the crisp notes with his thumb, he tried to estimate their total value, but he was far too flustered for such a calculation. Shaking his head, he put the envelope on the mantel and reached into the compartment for another. Then, against the background of the storm he heard a faint noise nearby. An instant later, the chandelier above him flooded the room with a harsh white light.

"You!" a voice exclaimed.

In the relative stillness the single word was like the blast of a trumpet.

Blinded by the glare and feeling a terrible coldness around his heart, the youth flinched and backed against the chimney. Suddenly his legs were flaccid. Suddenly his mind ground to a halt, and his nervous system began to twitch and jerk as though galvanized. Merely to turn his head in the direction from which the voice had come demanded a Herculean effort of determination. He made that effort and saw through a dazzling haze Louise Vaughan standing by the half-open double door. A light coral-colored robe was thrown over her slim shoulders; beneath it she wore a short, pink, transparent camisole. Her face was flushed with recent sleep, her eyebrows arched and her mouth fixed in a sardonic smile.

"Who would have thought it?" she said, surprise giving a lilt to the words.

Osgood blinked and opened his mouth, but didn't say anything.

"Such a clean-cut type," the woman continued. "So young, so wholesome, so innocent, so straight of limb and proud of carriage."

"I . . . I . . . I figured everybody was . . . was in bed," he stuttered through quivering lips.

"No doubt, Edward, no doubt," she replied gently. "And we were too, but I was awakened by the banging of a shutter—and when I went to fasten it I thought I heard a window being surreptitiously raised down here. How in the world did you fathom that mantelpiece? Richard believes it's absolutely foolproof. Even I don't know exactly how it works, though Nigel tried to explain it to me one time."

Hearing the lunatic's name, Osgood stopped biting his lower lip and rubbing his palms on his blue jeans. Into his frightened and bewildered brain the rudiments of an idea drifted. "Nigel," he blurted out. "Nigel told me how to do it. Nigel gave me the secret, Mrs. Vaughan."

She flashed a quizzical look. "Are you saying he put you up to it?" she inquired in a dulcet tone.

"Right . . . right. That's it exactly. He . . . he wanted his coin collection—and he told me it was kept here."

"But it's one o'clock in the morning, dear."

"Yes, but . . . but he said he didn't want his brother to know. He said the coins were valuable, and his brother wouldn't let him have them because . . . he might lose them."

"I see. How could he lose them in his prison, though?"

Osgood wagged his head, then shrugged his shoulders. "I don't know. Maybe he'd drop them out the window or something."

"Yes, that's a possibility, isn't it? And have you found them?"

"The coins? No, they're not in the safe. There's some gold coins, but Nigel's were supposed to be silver. He must've lied to me, Mrs. Vaughan."

The sardonic smile returned to the woman's lips. She stepped into the room and closed the door behind her, saying, "What a curious story."

Now that his eyes had adjusted to the light he could see her more clearly—could even see the features of her thin body beneath the sheer nightgown. But he could also detect tne total disbelief that was imprinted on her face.

"The only reason I agreed to do it was on account of his mood," he declared rapidly, as if his plausibility depended on the velocity of his speech. "Lately he's been very dejected, and I thought it would cheer him up some. He said the coin collection was the only thing in the safe, but cripes! Now I see there's a lot of other stuff there—papers, books, envelopes."

"And money," Louise added, leaning against the side of a chair and regarding him with amused eyes. The camisole, ending where her legs began, scarcely covered her torso. "I don't believe a word of it, Edward, although I must admit you're a resourceful liar," she went on cheerfully. "I couldn't have thought up anything nearly so clever at such short notice."

"I'm not lying, Mrs. Vaughan," Osgood protested, coming out from behind the mantelpiece to better plead his case. "I swear I'm not lying."

"No? Well, perhaps you aren't. Should we call your uncle down and ask him what he thinks of it all?"

The youth let his eyes drop from her face to her feet, shod in coral leather slippers with wedge-shaped heels. "He won't believe me any more than you do," he replied weakly.

"Not necessarily, dear," she rejoined. "We could go to the cottage and speak to Nigel, couldn't we? And if he corroborates your story, then your innocence"—she lingered over the word—"would be proven beyond a doubt."

"I'm confused, Mrs. Vaughan," Osgood said in a plaintive voice, his whole expression one of abject misery. "I can't think straight. Maybe Nigel tricked me. Maybe he just sent me on a wild-goose chase, because...because the coin collection isn't really in there. And when we go to talk to him, he might deny everything."

"But why would he want to do a nasty thing like that, Edward?"

"Because he's crazy—and he's mad at me, too. A couple of weeks ago, we had a fight. That's why I called Uncle Richard in Providence that night. And Nigel's the kind of person who bears grudges." Osgood brought his eyes up again and looked at the woman directly. "I'm scared, Mrs. Vaughan. I don't want to go to jail," he said tremulously.

A blast of wind buffeted the front of the house. The rain beat a sharp tattoo on the windows in the bay, and there was a general creaking of the old building's joists, floor boards, and beams. Louise inclined her head slightly, as though she were listening with the greatest interest to this eerie tumult. When it subsided she walked slowly toward him, her fair legs reflecting the chandelier's glow.

"I can understand that," she said, coming to a halt quite close to him. "For a virile and vigorous young man—and you fit that description nicely, in my opinion—imprisonment would be an ordeal, a tragedy, a waste."

Hearing these words and the tender tone in which they were conveyed, Edward Osgood felt hope kindling in his breast where before there had been only icy terror. "It would kill me. I'm sure of it, Mrs. Vaughan," he said, letting his eyelids droop a quarter of an inch.

"It might, although you're obviously very strong," she declared. "Of course, whether or not you go to jail depends on me, doesn't it?"

He nodded, then bowed his head.

"And if I said nothing about it, dear—if I made it our little secret, this burglary in the night—would you be grateful to me?"

"Yes, Mrs. Vaughan—tremendously grateful."

"Ah," she sighed. "But how grateful is tremendously grateful, Edward? Would you be my vassal? My slave?"

By now the woman was so close to him that he could see the rather coarse texture of her tousled blonde hair, smell the scent she used, and feel her warm breath on his cheek. "Yes," he answered, "I would."

"Forever?" she murmured, putting her hand on his shoulder.

"Forever," he conceded, as he threw his arms around her slight form, drew her to his chest, and kissed her mouth with fervor.

Louise Vaughan's response did not lack enthusiasm, but after a comparatively short time she tilted her head back, peered up at him through gray eyes that were slits, and said reproachfully, "Is this your notion of servile behavior, dear?"

"Sure," he replied with a grin that was both broad and lewd. "It's what you wanted me to do, isn't it?"

"What a cocky son-of-a-bitch!" she said, raising her eyebrows. "So young, yet so crammed with egotism."

"Not egotism, just confidence," he said, bending forward to kiss her again.

"But how can you be confident, under the circumstances?" she asked, tantalizing him by averting her face.

"I guess because I'm young and vigorous, Louise," he said, pressing his lips to her ear, which was the only part of her head he could get at. Then, as an afterthought, he added, "Not that age matters."

74

"Ah, I see. You don't mind a lady as mature as I am—is that it, Edward?"

"I don't mind at all. There's no substitute for experience, is there? Elderly women know the movements—and they don't have a lot of hang-ups like . . ."

"Elderly?" she yelped, pushing his chest with her hands. "Elderly? Aren't you gallant! How old do you think I am? Perhaps with my long and extensive experience I'm taking advantage of you."

"I'm not complaining, Louise. Let's sit on the rug," he suggested, slipping his hand inside the open robe to caress her bare buttocks. "We'll be more comfortable there."

The woman's body stiffened in his arms, but Osgood was by this time so aroused that he didn't notice. "I think not," she said frigidly. "Let go of me, slave."

"It's a soft rug," he said, touching her ear with the tip of his tongue. "Almost like a feather bed."

"I don't care if it's wall-to-wall goddamned mink," she retorted, her voice rising in volume and pitch. "Let go of me, please."

Encircling her waist with the arm that wasn't beneath the robe, he started to kneel and to pull her down with him. She struggled in his grasp, exclaimed, "Get your paws off me, Edward!" and then hit him on the nose with her fist.

Though the blow wasn't very sharp—hardly more than a light jab—it landed on a sensitive spot and brought tears instantly to the youth's eyes. "You bitch!" he snarled in surprise. "Who the hell do you think you are?"

"Me? I'm the elderly lady who can put you in prison, you damned conceited little sneak thief," she told him loudly. "And when at last you get out of there, Lochinvar, you'll be a hell of a lot older than I am."

Osgood's pain faded swiftly, but his anger, aggravated by her scornful remarks, did not fade with it. And to worsen the situation, because of all the noise she was making, he was becoming frightened again. He straightened up, turned her around roughly, and clamped his hand over her mouth—but she promptly bit the edge of his palm and drove her elbow into his ribs. This new anguish did nothing to diminish his rage. He swore and yanked his hand away, and when he did that she shrieked, "Richard!" at the top of her lungs.

A tidal wave of panic inundated his brain and drowned his reason. Wrapping his arm around her throat he forced her chin up and her head back. When she attempted to scream again, he tightened his hold and bent her over his out-thrust hip. Only a wheezy gurgle came from her gaping mouth.

"For God's sake, be quiet," he said in a kind of imperious whine. "Take it easy, Mrs. Vaughan. Calm down. Calling him in won't help matters. No . . . no. Don't you see? He'll get the wrong idea. I mean, you haven't got much clothing on, and I could always say you invited me here. Sure, Louise, sure. I could even tell him you were the one who opened the safe, because you wanted to give me a little money as a gift. You understand what I'm saying? And Uncle Richard would believe me, because as you said yourself, I'm a pretty good liar. I only have to unbuckle my pants, and it'll look just like a scene from a skin flick. So don't go making a fuss, Louise. Take it nice and easy. Stay cool. You've got a lot more to lose than..."

The sentence died in Osgood's throat. Suddenly it dawned on him that he was supporting the woman's whole weight. Looking down he could see her two small feet in their coral slippers dangling several inches above the floor. She had stopped wriggling, and he could feel the total limpness of her body against his own.

"Louise!" he whispered, sliding his hands under her arms and spinning her about, in order to see her face. The delicate features were strangely dark, the gray eyes closed. "Are you okay, Mrs. Vaughan?"

Not with a word or a groan, not with the faintest wrinkling of her brow or the flicker of an eyelash, did she answer. Her lips were noticeably slack, and heliotrope in color. Through the crevice that separated them, he could distinguish two small teeth that glistened like pallid gems.

"Are you okay?" he repeated with rising urgency.

Taking her up in his arms, he carried her to a red brocade wing chair a few feet away, and when he set her in it, her blonde head drooped onto her shoulder like the head of an unstrung marionette.

"Fainted . . . passed out. That's all," he assured himself in a hoarse undertone, as he pressed his ear beneath her left breast and listened anxiously. No sound whatever came from within. "It's the storm. I can't hear because of that damned wind."

But there wasn't any pulse in her thin wrist, either, nor any indication that she was breathing. Meanwhile, her complexion appeared to grow duskier.

"God!" he gasped. "My God!" Frantically he pulled the woman out of the chair and onto the floor. "Wake up, damn you!"

Then, like a lover in the throes of an excruciating passion, he fixed his mouth against hers and tried desperately to blow life back into her lungs. But at the end of many minutes, with his own lungs aching and the sweat running down his face, he was compelled to acknowledge defeat. The body of Louise Vaughan remained inert and inanimate.

Osgood, growling like an animal, hauled her once again into the red wing chair, raised one of her eyelids and very deliberately jabbed the eyeball itself with his thumbnail. The action, however, extreme as it was, evoked no reaction. He might as well have stuck his finger in the eye of an effigy. And to make matters worse, when he released the eyelid it refused to close again, as if to demonstrate once and for all the unqualified lifelessness of its owner.

"Is it possible?" he asked in a hollow voice, stepping back and aimlessly scanning the room. "Dead? How could it happen?" But the bookcases, the upholstered chairs, the long desk, and the mantelpiece still protruding grotesquely from the wall were not able to supply the answer he sought. "I only put my arm around her . . . hardly even touched her. How could it happen?"

Taking a few faltering steps into the center of the room, he contemplated with haunted eyes the silvery rivulets of rain on the trembling bay windows, grimaced, cursed, exhaled all his breath in a hissing rush, and clutched his head in both hands. A moment later, having become acutely conscious of his conspicuous position, he ran to the door and switched the chandelier lights off. Absolute gloom descended on him, bringing with it an exaggerated sense of security, a feeling of being quite invisible to the world. Then suddenly a bolt of lightning creased the black sky outside the window and bathed the den in a cold and garish gleam. By it he saw the winking Louise sprawled in the armchair like a lascivious rag doll. Her blonde hair was in disarray, her gown half off her shoulders, her flimsy pink nightgown pushed almost to her hips. This illumination lasted only a second, however, and the thick sheltering darkness, to his relief, closed down upon him again.

Groping blindly, he made his way to the mantel and picked up the bulging envelope on it, just as the thunder exploded over the rooftop. He flinched and shuddered. But, even while the rumbling echoes were fading, he returned the money to the rectangular hole and shut the steel door. Minutes later he had the mantelpiece back where it belonged, the carvings lowered on the half-pillars, the picture hook rotated, and the picture itself once more hanging on the wall. While he performed these chores he several times glanced towards the wing chair, hoping against hope that he would see a shadowy movement there. But Mrs. Vaughan didn't stir.

Now that he had done something positive he became calmer, however. His brain began to operate in a near-normal manner, so that for the first time he could comprehend his predicament with a degree of clarity.

"You have to hide her somewhere," the plausible voice inside his skull murmured. "In the cellar, maybe? Or out in one of the sheds?"

"No . . . no," he answered. "They'd find her. When they miss her, they'll go looking."

"Then bury her in the sand—or, better still, throw her into the ocean."

"The ocean," he repeated, staring at the figure slumped in the chair.

"Right," said the voice, now full of confidence. "Suppose she decided to go for a walk on the beach to watch the storm? And a big wave came up and swept her into the water. Yes, suppose she was drowned?"

"It could happen that way," Osgood whispered.

"Sure, sure. She liked to go down to the beach at night, didn't she? It's made to order. But you'll have to get her a coat or a jacket. She wouldn't go in her nightgown, not in weather like this," the voice argued slyly.

With his eyes now accustomed to the dark, the youth was able to hasten to the door without crashing into anything, and when he opened it, he found the feebly lighted hall as tranquil as an empty chapel. He tiptoed out, crept around the corner to the vestibule, and quietly let himself into the cloakroom. There, on a row of wrought-iron hooks, were odds and ends of clothing, hats, umbrellas, and beach bags. As he looked everything over, his eyes alighted on an orange cardigan that lay folded on a shelf in the corner. Across its breast pocket the name *Nigel* was embroidered in blue thread. Osgood frowned at it for a moment, and then, despite all his apprehensions, grinned.

"Why not?" the voice in his head asked excitedly.

From the rack he chose a small blue raincoat and a plastic hat that almost matched it, and from an assortment of clogs, sandals, tennis shoes, and other footwear on the floor, he selected a pair of ankle-high vinyl rubbers. For good measure, he took along a lady's yellow umbrella.

When he got back to the den, the luminous dial of an onyx clock on the mahogany desk showed the time to be exactly a quarter to two.

Though he was a husky young man in the best of shape, and his grisly burden weighed only a hundred pounds, Edward Osgood's journey down the steep hillside was by no means an easy one. Lashed by the cold wind, pelted by the icy rain, tripped up in the stygian murk by tufts, roots, rocks, and vines, he was fortunate to reach his destination without breaking a leg.

Under cover of a peal of thunder he opened the cottage door, entered, and hurried past Adriana's apartment. Up the stairs he staggered, the chilling rain and hot perspiration streaming the length of his backbone beneath his heavy sweater. At the landing outside his room he placed the dead woman on the floor, leaned exhausted on the newel-post, and listened intently. Above the sound of his own heavy breathing, only the howling of the gale was audible.

After a few minutes he again lifted the body and, moving as silently as circumstances would allow, he went through the pantry and into the corridor. There he paused a second time, until the hum of Nigel's peaceful snoring told him it was safe to continue. By the feeble nightlight in the baseboard, Osgood carefully lowered the limp form to the carpet directly in front of the lunatic's living-room door, unbuttoned the blue raincoat, removed the plastic hat and tossed it on the swivel chair, and propped the yellow umbrella against the desk. At some point in the hectic trip, Louise's eye had finally closed, and she now

80

looked almost contented. He returned to the landing and, with a rag from the pantry, wiped away the puddles of water he and the corpse had left there.

Satisfied at last, he straightened up and started for his room. Then he saw Adriana watching him from the floor below.

· 16 ·

Osgood, until that instant, had every reason to believe the worst part of his ordeal was over. He had carried out an extremely difficult job with ingenuity and courage. No professional assassin who disposed of cadavers on a regular basis could have done better. He had coolly dressed the pliant body in a coat, patiently worked the slipper feet into the overshoes, jammed the hat on the blonde head, hoisted the gruesome bundle to his shoulder, climbed out the bay window, and fled from Grayhaven. He had even been crafty enough to stop at the edge of the lawn and smear mud on his victim's vinyl boots, to make it appear she had walked through the rain. And when he had finished his strenuous trek and entered the cottage, he had rid himself of the body in a very clever fashion. He had acted decisively and kept his nerve throughout, but now, seeing the nurse at the foot of the stairs gazing up at him with horror-filled eyes, all confidence leaked from his heart and sinews like water from a cracked jug. Had the girl been a Gorgon, gifted with the power to turn people to stone by the force of her scrutiny, he could not have stood more immobile.

"What happened?" she asked in a voice faint with emotion.

"You've been watching," he said dully.

She nodded a single time. "What happened to her, Ned?"

Osgood ransacked his tired brain for an answer that might mitigate the harsh reality of the corpse down the hall, but there was none to be found. After a minute's agonized silence, he whispered, "She died."

"How, Ned?"

"How? I don't know. She must've had a stroke ... yes, or a fit, or a heart attack. Something ... quick."

Puzzled, Adriana frowned. "Where was she? I don't understand. Did you go to meet her?"

"No, no. Meet her? Of course not," he replied quickly. "I heard this noise—a call for help. So ... so I ran out, and there she was lying in the grass."

"But you've been gone nearly an hour, Ned."

"That's a lie, Adriana," he snapped fiercely. "It's not true. What are you saying?"

The girl ascended the stairs, gripping the banister with one hand and holding her flowered bathrobe closed with the other. When she stood before him she said, so softly that he could hardly hear her, "You went to meet that woman, didn't you?"

"Christ, that's ridiculous ... crazy," he answered, shaking his head violently and sending a spray of rainwater in all directions. "There wasn't anything like that going on. I swear to God."

"I saw you leave. I saw you climb the hill. I saw the light come on in the house."

He reached out to grasp her by the shoulders—then, remembering how he had seized Mrs. Vaughan, he dropped his hands in guilty fear. "No, I didn't. I didn't. I didn't," he chanted desperately. "You must have imagined it."

"And did I imagine that you brought her to the cottage dead, and put her in there?" she asked, indicating the direction she meant with an infinitesimal flicker of her sad hazel eyes.

Suddenly Osgood realized just how absurd his story was. The girl's arrival had thrown him into a state of shock. He was rambling on like a geriatric. If Louise had died naturally, what possible reason could he have for dumping her in the corridor? If there was nothing to hide, why hadn't he simply called the nurse or phoned the mainhouse for assistance? He was talking nonsense—spouting anything that came into his head in order to avoid telling the truth. But the truth would have to be told to Adriana. Sickness and death were her business, and once she saw Louise's face she'd know immediately how the woman had lost her life. To survive the catastrophe he would have to reveal the whole miserable affair, reveal it and beg for her cooperation.

The color drained from his face, and his broad shoulders sagged. He turned, pushed his door open, shambled into the room, switched the lamp on and looked with no real interest at his alarm clock. It was ten past two. She followed him in, shutting the door quietly. Together they sat down on the side of the bed, his expression one of grim stupefaction, hers of grief and concern.

"They'll lock me up for life," he mumbled.

"What did you do, Ned? Tell me," she implored. "Tell me."

The last of his self-possession gone, Osgood bowed his head and did as he was asked. Rueful words poured from his lips. He described the whole adventure from its impulsive beginning to its disastrous end, altering only a single detail—that he had tried to make love to Mrs. Vaughan. The woman had offered herself to him, he asserted, even tried to blackmail him into submitting, but he had resisted her advances. Then she started to scream and make a fuss, and he had grabbed her because he was frightened. But he had only put his arm around her. He never intended to do her any harm. Yet she died. One minute she was yelling at him, and the next she was dead.

Adriana remained mute for some little while after he had finished his story, while the youth watched her covertly from the corners of his eyes. Finally, she commenced to cry. Encouraged by this reaction, Osgood patted her knee and made soothing noises.

"It's horrible, Edward—horrible," she said between sobs. "It's so sordid. She caught you stealing, and you murdered her."

"Adriana, it was an accident. I hardly touched her," he answered dejectedly. "I had her in a kind of headlock, but it wasn't tight. The next thing I knew she collapsed. It wasn't murder, Adriana. It was an accident. There was something wrong with the woman, because I hardly touched her. I swear."

"And afterwards?"

"What do you mean?"

"How did you act afterwards? You brought her here, didn't you?"

"Sure. I had to."

"So you could put the blame on Nigel?"

"Yes—and why not? What difference does it make to him, Adriana? He's already a murderer, isn't he? And since there's no death penalty any more, what can they do to him? Nothing. But if they nail me for it, they'll stick me away for twenty years. Twenty years! I couldn't take that. Never. I can't stand being boxed in, cooped up, trapped. It would kill me. Look . . . don't you understand? I went there for the money, because that way we could've gotten married sooner. I wanted the money for our future. I figured Uncle Richard doesn't need it. So you have to help me. You have to keep quiet—not say anything. Believe me, Adriana, this scheme will work. Louise was a freaky woman, a kook. She came to see him and he grabbed her. Wasn't he always raving about her? Nigel had a crush on his brother's wife, right? It works out perfectly, don't you see?"

"His brother's wife?" she asked in a curious tone.

"Yes—Louise, Louise," he said impatiently.

"But Louise wasn't Richard's wife. She was Nigel's."

"Nigel's? What are you talking about?"

"Louise was Nigel's wife. I thought you knew that.

He married her fifteen or sixteen years ago."

"But . . . but how the hell could she marry Nigel? The guy's a total cuckoo. Do you mean they actually lived together?"

"Yes," said the girl vaguely. "For a couple of years. It was a lucid period for him. He was quite calm, they told me. He was even writing a book—a book of essays."

"Why did she marry him, Adriana? They're so different."

"I believe he had come into some money, at the time. His mother had established a trust for him that he got at the age of thirty."

Osgood looked at her sharply. "That was it, then. She did it for money. And afterwards she became Richard's girl friend?"

"Yes. Most people assumed she was his wife because they had the same last name, I guess, while those who knew she wasn't wouldn't see anything wrong with her coming here so often, since it was where her ill husband lived."

The youth digested this revelation, and said, "What a bitch! She's messing around with her husband's brother, while the poor sick clown is in there turning to a vegetable? Some people have no morals at all. And Uncle Richard is just as bad. Imagine doing something like that to your own flesh and blood." The youth grimaced in disgust, then added, "But it doesn't weaken my plan, does it? Actually it gives Nigel an even better motive. He killed her because he was jealous. Beautiful. Do you see, Adriana? It's foolproof—unless you give me away."

The yellow lamplight played on the nurse's drawn features, gilding her brow and cheekbones but leaving her eyes in deep shadow. "It isn't fair," she said flatly. "Who knows what they'll do to him? Who knows how Richard will react? It isn't fair . . . isn't right."

"Oh come on! Nigel's in jail already. Nothing's going

to happen to him. He's safe and secure. I'm the one who's in danger. I'm the person who'll be destroyed if you spill the beans."

"But, Ned, it's so dishonest and so cruel. I couldn't . . ."

"Okay," Osgood snapped. He closed his eyes tightly as though in great torment, and leaned back on the bed. "Okay. I figured you'd look at it that way. When my luck goes bad, it goes bad a hundred percent." As he said this he became aware of a hard, lumpy object pressing against his flank, and realized it was the antler handle of his knife. Very deliberately he slid his hand beneath his body. "But I'm not going to go to prison. Not me, Adriana. I'll kill myself first," he declared in a harsh and desperate tone.

With a sudden, violent movement he brought his hand back in view, and the girl saw the knife just as he flicked it open. She jumped up from the bed in alarm.

"Kill myself," he repeated wildly, resting the point of the long, tapered blade on his chest above his heart.

"No, Edward—no!" she begged.

"I'd rather be dead and buried than stuck in some stone room to rot," he exclaimed, scowling hideously.

"Don't, Ned. Put it away. Please," Adriana beseeched, extending a trembling hand towards him. "I'll do what you ask—anything. I'll tell them whatever you want, only put the knife away."

Osgood opened his troubled eyes and regarded her gravely. Out over the sea a ragged streak of lightning slashed the dark clouds, and seconds later the sound of crackling thunder invaded the quiet room. Osgood lifted the knife an inch, held it in that position for a few uncertain moments, and then with a soft groan tossed it to the foot of the bed.

Relieved, the nurse said, "It'll be all right." She attempted a smile. "Everything will be all right."

"But can you handle it?" he asked wearily.

"Yes, yes."

"You only have to say you didn't hear anything—that you slept straight through the night."

"But won't Nigel deny . . ."

"Sure. Who's going to believe him, though? God, the man's a homicidal maniac," said the youth, sitting up. "And stop worrying about him. The worst that can happen is that he'll be sent to an asylum on the mainland, which is exactly what he wants because he can escape from an asylum."

He leaned forward with his elbows on his knees and concealed his face in his hands. The rasp of his breathing mingled with the whistling wind that blew about the cottage chimneys.

"Everything will be all right," she said again, trying to convince herself as much as him.

"If you don't bitch it up," he said.

"I won't, Ned."

He lowered his hands and shot her a hostile glance. "Are you sure you can do it, Adriana? My life depends on it, you know."

"Yes, yes," she replied miserably, sitting back down beside him. "I won't make any mistakes. I'll help you, because I love you. I'll do whatever you want, Edward. Don't be angry with me. You know how much I love you."

The girl embraced him ardently, and with tears streaming from her eyes and pathetic little sobs from her lips, covered his cheeks and mouth with kisses.

They remained in each other's arms for more than a quarter of an hour. Then Osgood, after sternly repeating his instructions, sent her back to her apartment.

The rain began to slacken and the wind to die as he stripped off his damp clothing and crawled into bed, wondering uneasily where he would be sleeping the next night.

Intending to discover the body himself, Edward Osgood set his alarm for an early hour, but so fatigued was he by the night's harrowing events and heavy exertions that when it rang he turned it off with an oath and promptly fell back to sleep again. Not until five past eight did he reawaken. A hot shower and a hasty breakfast, though they helped greatly to revive him, delayed his departure for another half-hour. He had his hand on the doorknob when a wail of anguish came from the far side of the cottage. Beginning as a low vibrant moan, it ascended slowly in both pitch and intensity, continued for some moments at a shrill, nerve-tingling level, then ceased abruptly.

A shiver scuttled the length of Osgood's spine. "He's spotted her," he muttered, throwing open the door.

Hurrying across the landing, he ran through the pantry. Louise Vaughan lay on the carpet just as he had left her six hours earlier, her mottled face starkly limned by the ashen daylight that shone from the corridor windows. Nigel's bloodless countenance was pressed against the bars of the slot in the living room door. He seemed stunned.

Osgood, pretending surprise and dismay, rushed to the dead woman, dropped to one knee, and tried to raise her head, but the corpse, now quite rigid, came up in a solid, unjointed mass. The nape of her neck was as hard and cold as metal, while her still-damp blonde hair clung to his arm with the disagreeable tenacity of clammy seaweed. Overcome by sudden revulsion, he pulled his hands away from her—the lifeless skull hit the floor with a nasty thud.

"Dead," he declared, wiping his palms on his blue jeans.

"Dead," Nigel echoed in a sepulchral voice.

A period of eerie silence ensued during which both

men regarded the crumpled figure with manifest concentration, but then the clatter of footsteps in the pantry put an end to the quiet, and Adriana appeared in her flowered robe.

"I heard a cry," she said, avoiding Osgood's eyes. "Is something wrong? Who's that on the floor?"

"Dead. Louise is dead," Nigel intoned.

"What?"

"Yes. It's true. It's Mrs. Vaughan," said Osgood, standing up again. "I'd better phone Uncle Richard."

The nurse made a rapid examination of the body, touching the dark forehead and sunken cheeks, and glancing under the raincoat.

"She's been strangled," Nigel said dolorously. "That's why her complexion isn't fair any more. Somebody choked her. Suffocation deprives the blood of oxygen and turns the victim blue. I myself have seen that color before. Somebody killed her, Adriana—strangled the life out of her. Somebody killed Louise, but it wasn't me." The lunatic paused, uttered a hoarse sob, and began picking at the collar tab of the orange-checked sport shirt he was wearing. "Why would I do it? She was my beautiful wife. See how purple her lips are, Adriana? Cyanosis. As a registered nurse, you know what that is. A discoloration of the skin, due to an oxygen deficiency. Somebody strangled Louise . . . my Louise."

Having delivered this mournful monologue, Nigel retreated from the oak door and sat in his armchair. He stretched his long legs out before him, threw his head back, and contemplated the ceiling—contemplated it with half-closed eyes, as though it were a hundred miles away.

"Deplorable," Leon Perth said, wagging his red head and nervously wringing his hands. "It's a tragedy for all of us. Poor, poor Louise. Whatever possessed her to come here alone—and in the middle of the night? A mystifying, baffling question, that I suppose will never be answered. The rain didn't start until early morning, Richard, so it must have been late. Look, her coat is sodden, and she brought an umbrella. But with that wind I doubt that the umbrella was of much use. For a while I heard a shutter banging. Then it stopped, and I concluded that it had blown away. Under the coat, she's only wearing her nightclothes."

"I can see that," Vaughan said huskily.

Perth, detecting a note of censure in his employer's tone, responded apologetically, "I only meant she must have decided to come down on the spur of the moment. Maybe she was worried about him ... because of the violence and ferocity of the storm."

The four of them stood in a rough semicircle around the corpse, though only the politician persisted in looking at it. Osgood, his mouth firmly set in a sorrowful line, kept his eyes on a spot on the rug. He longed for time to pass swiftly, longed to have the whole terrible episode behind him.

If it were tomorrow, he thought, I'd be so damned happy. And if it were next week—or, better still, next month—I wouldn't ask for anything more for the rest of my life.

"Should I cover her face?" Adriana inquired timidly.

"Please do," Vaughan replied, his voice cracking on the second word.

The nurse went into the storeroom, returning a moment later with a bedsheet that she carefully spread over the body.

"What I simply cannot grasp or comprehend," Perth said ponderously, "is why nobody heard her enter. She had to pass by both your doors. And when she arrived here in the corridor and ... and the tragedy occurred, there must have been some struggle, some outcry. Louise was a spirited woman. She would not have surrendered or capitulated without a battle. No, sir. Yet neither of you heard a sound. It's difficult to understand."

"I suppose the racket of the storm . . ." Osgood began.

"Then you heard that noise, Edward? The storm awakened you?"

"Not completely, Leon. I knew it was raining and blowing, and the thunder disturbed me, but I never really woke up."

Perth left off wringing his hands and waved one of them in a gesture of annoyance. "Storm or no storm, a scream in a building as small as this should have been heard by someone. Your room is just down the passageway a few yards. And weren't you hired to watch him, you and Adriana? I should have thought that between the two of you this savage and senseless attack, this brutal slaying, could have been prevented. The poor woman was throttled virtually on your doorstep, Edward. Really, you must sleep like Rip Van Winkle."

Vaughan raised his eyes from the shrouded figure on the floor to the peevish face of his secretary, and said, "You talk too much, Leon."

"Sorry, Richard. It's just that I'm so upset," the little man replied, folding his arms across his chest and tucking his small hands into his armpits. "Whatever are we going to do?"

"I'll have to phone some people," Vaughan said softly, as if thinking aloud.

"Should I call the Fairoaks police?" Adriana asked.

"No, no, no," he answered her sharply. "Do nothing of the kind. I'll see to everything myself, Miss Danziger."

Osgood cleared his throat and declared, "If you want to fire me, Uncle Richard, I won't complain. Leon is right, I guess. It was my responsibility. I was nearest. I should have heard her come up the stairs and cross the landing."

"It wasn't your fault, Edward," said Vaughan, without looking at him. "I don't expect you to patrol the halls at night. The precautions we took were reasonable, but they couldn't cover every eventuality. And it's possible Louise was deliberately quiet."

Mechanically he drew his silver cigar case from his pocket and removed from it one of the thin, yellowish brown cylinders of tobacco. Osgood ran to the desk and obtained matches from a drawer, while Perth watched him with a trace of a sneer on his face.

"Thank you, Edward," the politician said, when the cigar was duly lit. "Is that your radio in the drawer?"

"Yes, Uncle Richard. The headset's there, too. I use it all the time," Osgood said, wondering why they were discussing his radio with a corpse lying only a few feet away.

From behind the golden oak door, a baritone humming suddenly came. It wasn't loud but it rose and fell fitfully, as though the hummer couldn't quite recall how the melody went.

"He's singing," Perth said. "He's actually singing."

"It's a hymn—'O Darkest Woe,'" Adriana said.

"Nevertheless, it's inappropriate under the circumstances," said Perth, outraged.

With the cigar jutting from his clenched right hand, Richard Vaughan circled the body of his dead mistress and went to his brother's door. "Why did she come here, Nigel?" he asked, peering through the aperture. "What did she say to you?"

The lunatic, who was sitting cross-legged on the rug beside his plastic coffee table, left off humming and answered, "She didn't. Didn't come here, and didn't say anything to me."

"But she's right here, dead . . . strangled."

"Who, Richard?"

"Louise, Louise."

"Ah, yes . . . my little Louise."

"Why did she visit you?"

"I told you—she didn't. It would be lovely to think she braved that tempest to spend an idle moment or two in my company, but reason and experience—cruel masters, both—force me to reject such a fantasy. How swarthy her face has become! Did you notice? Death doesn't even respect beauty. A damned mindless vandal, death is. Why are you asking me these inane questions, when you know I wish to be alone?"

"Someone killed her, Nigel."

"Of course. Haven't I been saying just that, Richard?" Nigel hunched over his crossed legs, his pale blue eyes inscrutable. "I woke up this morning and there she was . . . there she was. That swarthiness tells the story. She's been choked—slain by persons unknown, as they say in the newspapers. And that's the mystery. Who would have dreamed she'd go in such a bizarre fashion? Louise had a quick tongue and perhaps a too pragmatic way of coping with life, but there was no real harm in her. She was as sweet as a flower. As sweet as a primrose or a morning glory."

Vaughan sucked on the cigar so hard that the sound was audible, then blew white smoke through the bars. "Don't lie to me, Nigel," he said with obvious restraint. "Tell the truth. Why did Louise visit you?"

"She didn't. She was brought here dead." The madman began picking his shirt collar again. "My darling Louise," he said laboriously. "My Astarte . . . my Scheherazade. Who made your face dark, eh? Who shut off your life, Louise? When I know the murderer, I'll make him . . ."

"The murderer? The murderer is you," Vaughan said angrily.

"No," Nigel said. "I wouldn't do that. I wouldn't hurt Louise. From the day I was born till now, she was my only happy memory. I might murder you or Leon. I might murder anyone—the whole damned world—but not Louise. And you know that, Richard, you know it perfectly well. Now that she's gone, what's to become of me? How will I be able to endure the future? And being insane already, even the solace of losing my mind is denied me."

"Are you joking?" the politician asked, his ruddy face growing redder still, and his eyes closing to slits.

"No, are you? Who could find comedy in so cowardly a crime? Only the assassin."

"You're the assassin, Nigel. Admit it."

"I would if it were true, but it isn't," Nigel replied, twisting the collar tab in his fingers. "I suspect that the killer is you, Richard. You did it, eh? And you're trying to foist the blame on me again, just as you did when we were boys."

The accusation hung in the air like smoke after the firing of a gun. Vaughan turned his back on the oak door, the muscles of his face as tight as metal coils. "I didn't bring my key," he said. "Where is the other one?"

Momentarily confused, Osgood asked, "The other key?"

"Yes, yes—to the door, Edward."

The youth scurried out to the pantry, snatched the long-shanked iron key from its hook, and returned with it in his hand.

"I want the radio," Vaughan said succinctly, pointing to the transistor in the desk drawer with his slender cigar.

Osgood nodded, and got it for him.

"Do you think it's wise to go in there?" Adriana asked anxiously. "Wouldn't it be better if . . ."

"Open it up, Edward," the politician commanded, interrupting her.

Leon Perth clasped his hands together and began to sidle down the corridor. "Do be careful, Richard," he warned. "Nigel's a maniac, remember. And he has the strength of a gorilla."

Though Osgood, too, was more than a little nervous, he feigned a cool indifference to impress his uncle, and inserted the key without hesitating. As he twisted it, he could see Nigel jump to his feet. At that instant the

94

clamorous music of a rock band—a twanging, rasping, pounding, jarring noise—burst upon them all with the abruptness of an exploding grenade.

"Turn it off!" Nigel shouted excitedly. "Turn it off."

"No," his brother replied, pushing the door open and advancing into the apartment, holding the bawling radio in front of him like a weapon.

"Turn it off or I'll kill you, Richard," the lunatic threatened, slapping his long-fingered hands over his ears.

But there was no conviction in his voice, and his faded blue eyes were glazed with terror.

"No, you won't. I'm not a helpless woman, you miserable bastard," said Vaughan, moving steadily across the room. "I'm not some poor frail creature, you damned mad dog."

Osgood followed warily, noticing as he had on other occasions how strange the atmosphere was in the apartment. Thick, stale, full of subtle human odors—it could only be the air of a prison or some other place of confinement. As he looked over the politician's shoulder he saw Nigel, face contorted by panic, make a headlong dash for the bedroom—but somehow the fleeing man's legs became entangled, and he lost his balance. Down he fell, in an awkward sprawl on the floor.

From the corridor, Adriana called, "Don't hurt him. He's terrified. The noise . . . he's liable to have a seizure."

Richard Vaughan took no notice of her plea, however. His lips tightened into a bestial grin that distorted every line of his countenance, and he raised the volume of the radio as high as it would go. Loud as the music had been, it was now infinitely worse. Like a searing wind from a blast furnace, it swept the small room. The pulsing uproar reverberated off the walls and ceiling in such a manner that it assaulted the senses from every direction simultaneously. Whatever meager melodic charm the composition might have had under ordinary conditions vanished at once. The rhythm and harmony, even the individual characteristics of the different instruments, were so enmeshed in their own echoes that the end result was total pandemonium.

Nigel flinched as though he'd been hit by a knout. Then he jammed his long index fingers in his ears, squeezed his eyes closed, and commenced moving his mouth in peculiar fishlike spasms. Opalescent bubbles of saliva formed on his lips. But if he was trying to speak, the radio's blare drowned his words completely. Twice he attempted to get to his knees, and twice he collapsed on his face. With this second failure he stopped trying, and began instead to writhe and wriggle on the carpet like some large wild animal brought down by a hunter's high-powered bullet.

Edward Osgood himself wanted to plug his ears and run from the apartment, the noise was that painful. How could those tiny speakers generate such a strong signal? he wondered. And why was it so jumbled up? Had he broken the radio somehow? Involuntarily the youth's glance swung to the door behind him, back to the world of relative quiet. There on the doorsill Adriana stood, her face livid, her bosom heaving in agitation, and her hands tightly clenched at her sides.

Vaughan was now towering over his prostrate brother, a curious expression of loathing and triumph stamped on his flushed features. Beads of sweat blossomed on his brow and dripped like tears onto his fleshy cheeks. He, too, seemed to be saying something, for his lips moved from time to time like a worshiper uttering a silent prayer. Watching him, Osgood felt suddenly contemptuous. Both of them are crazy, he thought. Both of them are soft as marshmallows.

How long the politician remained there tormenting his brother with the radio, Edward Osgood was never able to calculate afterwards. Time itself succumbed to the earsplitting din of the booming drums, jangling electric piano, stuttering woodwinds, shrieking trumpets, and howling guitars. Seconds passed for minutes, and minutes for hours. The youth began to feel disoriented. It was as if the noise had somehow projected them all into a different universe. When would it end? he wondered listlessly.

But it was Adriana who finally rushed forward and dragged the obsessed Richard Vaughan back out into the hall, and there switched off the transistor. Silence overwhelmed them. For a minute or more they did nothing but feast their ears on it, like half-drowned men gulping air.

Vaughan's evil expression faded away by degrees. He shook his head, blinked his eyes, mopped his forehead with a handkerchief, and stumbled toward the pantry waving his arms as if to clear a path through a dense fog. Leon Perth, murmuring a string of platitudes, hurried after his dazed master.

As for Nigel, he stayed where he was—eyes still closed, mouth still working, frame still writhing. If he was conscious of the clamor's end, he displayed no sign of it. Foamy saliva like meringue coated his mouth. Ropy mucous dribbled from his quivering nose. His face and neck were bright with perspiration, and under his arms there were black semicircles on the orange-checked sport shirt.

Impulsively Adriana Danziger started to run towards the stricken man, but Osgood, anxious to get away, grabbed her roughly and propelled her into the corridor. She was still protesting when he slammed and locked the heavy oak door.

He then deposited the radio in the desk, picked up Richard Vaughan's cigar, which was smoldering on the rug not a foot from the covered corpse, snuffed it out in the ashtray, exchanged a somber glance with the nurse, and, gripping her arm, guided her in the direction of the staircase. As they passed through the pantry, he hung the wrought iron key back on its hook.

18

When Perth and Osgood returned a half-hour later, Nigel was lying on his tubular cot with his head beneath his pillow. Except for an occasional nervous jactitation of his left leg, he might have been as dead as his wife outside the door. The shade was still drawn on the window, and the room was gray with shadow. On the night table the orange tennis ball lay, looking strikingly incongruous in so somber a setting.

Eager to be finished with a nasty assignment, the two men quickly lifted the rigid cadaver—Osgood bearing most of the weight—and carried it into the storeroom where they concealed it behind some stacked copies of *The New York Times* and a carton of paper towels. They then went back to the office on the ground floor, where Adriana, pale and slightly wild-eyed, sat very erect in her swivel chair.

"We'll need the basement key," Perth said, patting his temples with a neatly folded handkerchief.

"It's there," the nurse answered, pointing towards a flat brass key on the corner of her desk. "But I don't like it, Leon. I don't like any of it."

Osgood threw her a swift, sharp glance, but said nothing.

"Please!" Perth protested, grimacing as if in pain. "We've got problems enough. This simply isn't the time to become temperamental, Adriana. There's too much to be done."

"We could be arrested as accessories to a murder," she said in a tremulous voice. "I think Mr. Vaughan is making a mistake."

"Rubbish. For one thing lunatics can't be charged with murder, and Nigel's been certified," Perth answered caustically.

Osgood gave the girl another sullen look. "Uncle Richard has good reasons for doing it this way, Adriana."

"Indeed he does," the secretary affirmed emphatically. "Weren't you listening when he explained it all? Louise was his concubine, his lady friend. That being the case, the guardians of the law are certain to take a critical, or even hostile, view of the situation. This by itself would be sufficiently bad, but when the media gets wind of it the political career of Richard Vaughan—which, aside from personal considerations, represents years of labor by thousands of dedicated Americans and quantities of expended money beyond your ability to imagine—will be totally destroyed. Good God, Adriana, can't you understand what's involved? The so-called gentlemen of the press will crucify him, skin him alive, roast him over a slow fire. And they won't be satisfied until they've questioned our friend upstairs, and you've already heard the mad accusations he's flinging about. No, when a politician's mistress dies violently, he'd be a fool not to keep it a secret if he can."

The nurse rocked nervously in her chair. "They lived as man and wife," she said. "Now he's going to throw her into the ocean like a piece of garbage."

"This is a dire emergency—a crisis," Perth replied, vexation furrowing his brow. "Mr. Vaughan has to swallow his personal feelings, and we have to swallow ours. We can't afford the luxury of sentiment. Believe me, Louise herself would have approved of the scheme. She was a very practical, sensible woman."

"It's nice to be soft hearted," Osgood said, taking a wrinkled cigarette from a crumpled pack, "but sometimes a soft heart can bring you a lot of grief."

"Can it?" she asked him, an edge to her voice.

"Maybe I'm dense," said Perth demurely, "yet I really can't see what the fuss is about. It's not as if we have to dispose of the body ourselves. All that will be taken care of by the people who are coming over to Scarp tonight."

"Who are these people, Leon?" the girl demanded,

suspicion strong in her brown eyes.

"How the devil should I know? They're troubleshooters, political handymen—fellows who undertake unpleasant projects and don't ask embarrassing questions, I guess. What business of yours is it who they are, anyway?"

"It's my business because I'll be their accomplice," she said.

"Let's not get melodramatic. You won't even meet them, and they won't meet you. Really, there isn't a blessed thing to worry about. If some hick cop from the mainland comes over and asks a few questions, you only have to say that you haven't seen Louise for a couple of days. Just keep in mind that she disappeared tonight, and not last night—otherwise they'll wonder why we delayed in notifying them. But, of course, she actually is disappearing tonight, isn't she? There's nothing to be anxious about, Adriana. In a resort area like Fairoaks, drownings happen every other week during the season. Furthermore, the local police aren't going to be eager to step on Mr. Vaughan's toes. He commands too much respect in these parts."

Before the glib secretary could go on with his argument, there was a loud howl of anguish from the second floor. The three of them in unison looked up at the ceiling. Poignant but brief, the dismal wail was like the cry of some monstrous seabird.

"Christ! I hope we won't be listening to that all day," Osgood muttered, puffing on his bent cigarette.

"He's suffering," Adriana said wearily.

"True, but he brought it on himself, didn't he?" Perth answered, though there was a hint of uneasiness in his aspect. "I suppose if he doesn't behave we'll have to shutter his windows to keep his caterwauling from attracting attention. It wouldn't do to have the boatmen telling stories ashore. One thing I'm certain of—Mr. Vaughan is definitely not going to let the police interview him. So we

100

must adhere strictly to the line he laid down to us—that Nigel is a blithering simpleton, and that meeting strangers sends him into fits and convulsions. I have plenty of letters from medical men to support and verify this description."

"I can't see that there'll be any hitches," Osgood remarked.

"Neither can I, Edward," said the redheaded man. "You, Adriana, should be the last person to raise objections. Isn't Nigel your patient? And isn't it your duty to protect him from traumatic experiences? As a professional nurse, surely you recognize the need to take an ethical stand in this emergency."

She gave him a scornful sidelong glance, and said bitterly, "An ethical stand? If protecting Nigel from trauma is my duty, I didn't perform it very well this morning, did I? After what Mr. Vaughan did to him, it will be a miracle if Nigel doesn't deteriorate completely—actually become a blithering simpleton."

"That's what's bothering you, isn't it?" Osgood asked, cigarette smoke ascending from his lips like ectoplasm from the mouth of a medium. "You're worried about your patient. But Uncle Richard just got mad, and Nigel's done lots of worse things to other people. We all have to stick together, Adriana. If we don't, who knows what will happen?"

For some seconds the nurse regarded him sadly. At last she sighed and said, "Very well, Edward."

"Then it's settled?" Perth inquired.

"Yes. I'll do what I'm told, Leon."

"And you won't regret it, either," he said, giving her a confident grin as he took the brass key from the desk. "In a week the whole deplorable and tragic business will have faded away—become merely a bad memory. Life has its difficult moments, but they pass on like everything else. Shall we go, Edward?"

Osgood dinched his mangled cigarette in the abalone

shell, and declared offhandedly, "You haven't told her what Uncle Richard said . . . about the money."

"Oh, yes. It slipped my mind," the secretary replied, accompanying his words with a snicker as he glanced at the puzzled nurse. "In view of the extra burdens you and Edward have had to bear lately, I've been instructed by Mr. Vaughan to give you both a twenty percent salary increase, commencing this week."

Adriana lowered her eyes, averted her face, and blushed.

Perth waited expectantly for an expression of gratitude from the girl, then, realizing there wasn't going to be one, he shrugged, turned, and started for the door.

From a jumble of ancient luggage in the cottage cellar they extricated an iron-bound bow-topped trunk and hauled it out into the light.

"That should be large enough," said Perth. "There must be room for the rocks, too. Without them the poor woman might come back to us on the next tide, and we don't want that, do we?"

After they had dusted the trunk and checked it for address labels and other identifying marks, they left it with its lid open and returned to the pantry upstairs.

The corpse was even stiffer than it had been earlier, and maneuvering it proved an awkward task—especially since the secretary was both feeble and inept. Eventually, however, Louise was transported to the basement. There, further problems arose. In order to fit the body into the trunk they had to bend one arm and both legs, and, because of the advanced rigor mortis, this produced some disconcerting creaking and cracking. Perth grew pale as a sheet and seemed ready to swoon, but he recovered quickly enough once the job was over and the convex lid was shut.

Shortly after eleven that night, a motor launch approached the island from the direction of Narragansett and anchored close in to the shore on the north side where the dunes and escarpments were highest. Minutes later a dory carrying two men in yachting caps left her stern and moved across the choppy water to the shallow beach. The men dragged the boat onto the shingle, climbed the bluff, and strode purposefully towards the cottage, as though they had traveled that way a hundred times before.

Crouching in the darkness by his window, Osgood heard the crunch of their footsteps on the path and watched them as they came to the cottage door. Both were tall, husky individuals, and both wore black windbreakers. One carried a coil of heavy rope over his shoulder.

"Tough-looking dudes," the youth whispered to himself.

They entered, disappearing from his range of vision. When he saw them again they had the bow-topped trunk, well wrapped in rope, slung between them.

"Easy," the taller of the two cautioned, in a voice that was scarcely more than a hiss.

Then, grunting softly, they conveyed the improvised casket with its rigid and constricted occupant off into the gloomy night.

Fifteen minutes later, the coughing of the launch's engine reached Osgood's waiting ears. It persisted for a brief time, growing gradually less audible, until at last he could hear it no more.

· 19 ·

The Fairoaks Police Department, on being informed by the wealthy and influential owner of Scarp Island that one of his house guests had evidently drowned while swimming at night, promptly sent over a sallow-faced detective named Raymond Calderone. Though he knew most of the town functionaries, Vaughan hadn't met this one—but he greeted the man cordially and conducted him into the den, and there, with an appropriate display of shock and sorrow, tersely related the story of Louise's disappearance.

"My sister-in-law often took a dip before retiring," he began, seated behind his vast mahogany desk. "When we saw she hadn't slept in her bed last night, we went looking for her. I discovered her dress and towel on the beach. It was a terrible jolt."

Perth, installed in the red wing chair with his thin legs crossed, added glumly, "We brought the skiff around and made a thorough search of the shoreline. There was no sign of her, however."

The detective had crew-cut gray hair and pink-rimmed eyes that were set very close together. "No shoes?" he said.

"What?" Vaughan asked, perplexed.

"On the beach there was a towel and a dress. What about shoes?"

"Oh, yes, of course. Her sandals were there, as well. I've put the things in her room, if you'd like to see them."

"Won't be necessary," Calderone said, pulling a worn black notebook from the inside pocket of his rumpled suit-coat. "How good could she swim, Mr. Vaughan?"

The politician weighed the question briefly, then answered, "She had plenty of confidence ... still, I wouldn't call her a strong swimmer."

"Uh-huh. She wasn't unhappy, was she?"

"Depressed? No, no. Louise was basically a cheerful, down-to-earth individual, in spite of the fact that her husband—my brother, Nigel—is mentally ill. That circumstance certainly hasn't made her life easier, of course, but I'm sure none of her friends would think of her as potentially suicidal."

"Definitely not the type," Perth chimed in, shaking his red head.

The detective let his eyes rove from one man to the

104

other, then flipped open the notebook and thumbed the pages until he found some blank space. "Excuse me for asking," he said, "but did the lady have any reason for wanting to skip? For vanishing voluntarily?"

"None whatsoever," Vaughan replied, a note of reproach in his vibrant voice.

"It happens sometimes. Could she have gone ashore on her own, if she wanted to?"

"No. All our boats are accounted for."

Calderone plucked a ball-point pen from his breast pocket, and declared, "On the pier just now while I was waiting for my transportation, I got to talking to Davy Gibbs. He's an old guy on social security who does a lot of rod-and-reel fishing. Yesterday, it seems, he went out for stripers and didn't get back till late, and on his way in he claims he saw a cabin cruiser leaving Scarp. Around eleven-thirty or so."

Richard Vaughan frowned and said, "To the best of my knowledge, there were no boats about after dark. Flowers made his last trip hours before the sun went down."

"According to Gibbs it wasn't Flowers' launch. What he saw was a thirty-foot flybridge sedan—a Chris-Craft, maybe. It was anchored off the northern end of the island, and when it left it headed for the open sea. Davy couldn't figure out why they were going in that direction so late at night, or why they had moored where there are shoals when there was a well-lighted jetty only a few hundred yards away."

"I don't even know anyone with a boat of that description," said Vaughan suavely. "Did you hear a cruiser, Leon?"

"No, I didn't," Perth answered, "and I was awake until midnight."

Calderone smiled faintly. "Well," he said, "I have to admit Davy isn't the most reliable guy in these parts. Always takes a full jug of Seagrams Seven with him when

105

he goes out, and there's not much left in the bottle when he gets home. Fellows like that are liable to spot all kinds of things, from sea monsters to Russian submarines." He scribbled several lines in his notebook before asking, "Have you searched the house, Mr. Vaughan?"

"From attic to cellar—every room, every closet," the politician replied. "And we've looked every place else on the island, too. I can promise you, my sister-in-law is no longer here—poor woman."

"Okay, gentlemen. Thanks for your cooperation," said the detective. "Now, would it be all right if I had a word with the other people—your employees—to see if they can add anything?"

Vaughan acceded to this request, but mentioned that his brother was far too ill to be subjected to an examination, that both his physician and psychiatrist didn't want him to be disturbed in any way, and that, since he was confined to a small part of the cottage, he could have seen nothing useful. Calderone made no objections.

A short while after the master of the house and his secretary departed, Muldoon and his wife came into the den looking uneasy and resentful. They stated at once that they hadn't seen nor heard a thing during the whole of the night. The investigator did his best with them, but between their deafness and their obvious desire to avoid involvement, he got little for his pains.

Adriana was the next to enter the room. Though outwardly self-possessed, she was inwardly tense as a bowstring. When she sat down Calderone politely asked about her job, how long she'd been working on the island, where she had come from originally, where she had gone to school, and finally what she knew about Mrs. Vaughan and her sudden disappearance. To all these queries she gave concise, unhurried answers that seemed to satisfy her close-eyed interrogator.

For another ten minutes he chatted with the nurse, going over some of the statements she had made, and occasionally jotting notes in his battered black book. At the end of that period, he stood up, thanked her with a bow, and showed her out.

As they passed in the hall, Osgood nodded to Adriana and then sauntered through the double door. Once he stepped into the den, however, into that unlucky room that had been the setting of his great calamity, much of his equanimity deserted him. His eyes became restless and glided to the spot on the rug where Louise had lain, moved to the red brocade-covered chair in which he had propped her, darted to the chandelier that had illuminated everything so starkly, drifted to the painting of the mountains above the trick fireplace, swept past the huge desk to the bay window through which he had climbed in alone and climbed out with a dead body, and at last jerked back to the half-smiling man with the crew-cut hair who was inviting him to sit down.

Anxious to avoid the wing chair, Osgood sat at the end of a gray velvet sofa a short distance away.

"Where are you from, Edward?" Calderone inquired in a friendly manner.

"Providence," the youth said.

"Uh-huh. And you've been here how long?"

"Two months, about."

"Like it?"

"Sure. It's a good deal. You have to stay here night and day, of course, but the pay isn't bad and your room and board are all taken care of."

"Where did you work before you came here?"

"In . . . in a bar, in Cranston."

The detective's eyebrows, which were separated by less than a quarter of an inch, lifted infinitesimally.

Osgood said quickly, "I'm not a professional nurse, but Mr. Vaughan, who's my uncle, asked me to help out here so I came along. Actually I studied accounting at college . . . at U.R.I."

"Graduate, Edward?"

"Not yet. I'm short a few credits, but I'm going back to finish. Maybe next year. I had problems that ruined my concentration—money, a girlfriend ... that kind of thing."

Smiling sympathetically, Raymond Calderone steered the conversation to Louise Vaughan. Essentially, Osgood's story was the same as Adriana's. He hadn't encountered the woman the previous day, and didn't know she was missing this morning until Perth brought the news to the cottage. The people up at Grayhaven kept pretty much to themselves, he explained. As to the mysterious thirty-foot cruiser reported by the fisherman, he couldn't remember hearing any ships nearby late at night, and he certainly hadn't seen any strangers wandering around the island.

When questioned about Nigel, Osgood replied that his patient was almost an idiot and had to be looked after like a child, and that he had frequent and severe attacks of nervousness.

Calderone leaned forward in his chair and regarded him steadily. "Tell me," he said. "If Nigel's such a ding-a-ling, how come Louise ever married him, Edward?"

This sudden change of tack caught the youth off balance. He hesitated a moment before saying, "I don't know much about that. It happened a long, long time ago, when Nigel was in better shape."

"Yeah? How much better could he be? Feeble-mindedness doesn't hit you overnight like Asian flu. Usually it's a birth defect, or something you get in early childhood. And this Louise—she never struck me as the kind of woman who would go for a guy she had to spoon-feed every morning."

"You knew her?" Osgood asked in surprise.

"Only by sight. I used to see her on the pier. I hang around there to keep people from sailing away with other people's pleasure craft. Stolen boats is one of those growth industries. Mrs. Vaughan visited her husband often, huh?"

In the man's voice there was a hint of irony.

"Every couple of weeks," said Osgood, feeling more and more uncomfortable.

"Very devoted she must have been, which is kind of funny considering she really didn't look the type. I got the impression myself that Louise was cool and fast—a very hip broad. Something about the way she dressed and talked and moved." Calderone made more notations in his book, then raised his sallow face and grinned. "Are you sure she made all those trips out here just to see Nigel?"

But Osgood, alerted by what had gone before, was expecting the question. "Well, it's a nice place to visit," he said innocently. "I mean, there's the beach and the boats and everything."

"There's also her brother-in-law, isn't there?"

Osgood let his expression run from bewilderment to comprehension. "I wouldn't know about that," he said. "I hardly have any contact with the people at the mainhouse here."

"Maybe not, Edward, but you've got eyes like everybody else. Did Louise and Richard Vaughan behave in an intimate manner, would you say?"

"Intimate? They behaved like relatives, that's all."

"Husband and wife are relatives," the detective pointed out trenchantly.

"Well, they didn't act like husband and wife—not as far as I could see."

Calderone tapped his notebook with the end of the ball-point pen. He appeared dissatisfied. "When a doll like that goes missing off an island . . ." he began, then left the sentence unfinished. The room became very quiet. Suddenly he asked, "Ever been in trouble, Edward?"

"No, no. Trouble? What kind of trouble?" the youth

responded, a little too fast to sound natural.

"You know, with the law. Dealing grass or pills, fighting—anything like that?"

"Not really."

"What does that mean?" the policeman said sharply.

"I . . . I was arrested once for using somebody's car, but it was a big mistake. The car belonged to my girl."

"Did she know you took it?"

"Sure. She gave me the keys."

"How come she reported it stolen, then?"

"Because she was mad at me," said Osgood, his face growing red beneath his tan. "We had an argument."

"Did it go to court?"

"Yes, but the judge put me on probation. This was more than five years ago—and anyway it was all a stupid misunderstanding."

"A bum rap, huh? But you've got a felony conviction on your record, just the same," Calderone said, fixing him with his close-set, pink-rimmed eyes. "And it happened in Providence?"

"Right—East Providence, actually."

"Okay, Edward. That's it. If you hear anything interesting—anything that strikes you as suspicious—give me a call, won't you? I've got a strong hunch we're not going to find the lady's body. Maybe it's just as well. Your boss has a lot of clout, I understand. But I'm still in the market for information. So do me a favor, huh? Sometimes guys like you need help from guys like me. Keep your eyes and ears open."

Osgood left the den feeling relieved but groggy.

· **20** ·

"Conscientious, Leon, isn't he? But all the same it's a shameful waste of public revenue," the politician remarked in an amused tone.

110

His secretary, hovering at his shoulder, responded with an obsequious chuckle.

It was mid-afternoon, and they were standing at an upper window of Grayhaven, from which in the distance could be seen a dark blue police launch with a bright yellow emblem on its wheelhouse. The craft meandered slowly along the island's seaward shore. Seated on the windlass, and easily identifiable by his gray crew-cut head, was Raymond Calderone.

A short while later, when the launch rounded the point and came creeping down the western coastline, Adriana and Osgood also observed it with considerable interest from the youth's room on the second floor.

"Do you think he'll find anything, Ned?" the girl asked softly.

"No. How can he? There's nothing to find. He ought to give up and go home. Cops are dumb," said Osgood, sneering. "Doesn't he look like a moron, sitting out there in his crummy blue suit? I'll bet those guys last night took the body halfway to Europe."

Nigel, too, was paying close attention to the vessel's maneuvers. Eyes bloodshot from weeping, face haggard and ivory pale, the madman gazed through his opera glasses at the scene below, mumbling unintelligible words and phrases in a hoarse and broken voice.

Eventually, however, the blue launch with the yellow emblem abandoned its search. Veering about with a show of reluctance and leaving a silver crescent of wake on the dark water, it steered for Fairoaks.

Nothing more was heard from Detective Calderone for quite a while.

PART
TWO

PART TWO

Three days after the disappearance of Louise, Richard Vaughan and Leon Perth returned to the mainland and to those varied activities that men in public life are obliged to pursue. The story of the drowning was carried by the Fairoaks *Citizen*, the Providence *Journal*, and the Boston *Herald American*, but only as a short item of passing interest. Osgood, who had searched out all three articles, marveled that a human being could perish so mysteriously and not create the least stir in the world at large.

"You see, Adriana," he told the nurse with pride, "if you use your brains, you can solve any problem—any problem at all."

For the remainder of July the weather was unsettled, and while there were a few balmy days, there were many more damp and chilly ones. The torrid heat that had favored them in early summer had evidently left for other parts, abandoning the tiny island to cold drizzles and sudden squalls. And when the place was cut off from the rest of the planet by angry black clouds, curtains of rain, banks of mist, and the roaring tumbling Atlantic Ocean, it became a dim and desolate outpost—a lonely egg-shaped rock in the middle of nowhere.

The two young people made the best of it, however. In the evening they would bundle up and go for walks along the beaches, braving the wind, rain, and sea spray for the sake of exercise and nose-tingling fresh air. By an unspoken mutual consent, they avoided all mention of the recent tragedy, though the terrors of that stormy night were certainly not forgotten by either of them. Osgood, in spite of himself, would often survey the restless blue green water—gazing out to where the waves rose and fell with tireless regularity, half-expecting to see an iron-bound bow-topped trunk floating there amidst the whitecaps. Of course, except for the occasional chunk of driftwood or battered oil drum, he never spied anything—yet this didn't keep him from going on with his search. Aside from that, however, he seemed as care-free as before.

The death of Louise and its accompanying circumstances had a more noticeable effect on Adriana. She was seldom really light-hearted, seldom spontaneously happy. Like the fog that hung about Scarp Island, the nurse's appalling recollections of that ill-fated night and morning cast a mantle of shadow over her mind, depriving it of the sunny optimism that had once flourished there. Yet, strange to say, her feelings for Edward Osgood were more ardent than ever. She loved him with a hectic passion. It was as though the crime, for all its evil, had actually drawn her closer to the criminal. Nevertheless, being wiser than her paramour, she recognized that the grim secret they shared constituted a sinister and dangerous bond between them.

As for Nigel Vaughan, the person most affected by the sudden death of the blonde woman, he suffered greatly during this period. For hours he would lie on his cot crying, or sit in the armchair staring at the backs of his hands, or stand in the center of the room with his eyes tightly closed, or recline on the floor talking to himself in conspiratorial whispers. He wouldn't answer them when they spoke; he wouldn't eat his meals; he wouldn't shave or take a shower. Sometimes Osgood would catch him looking through the bars, glaring out at him, his eyes burning with hatred. One week Nigel wore an overcoat, an orange stocking cap, a pair of galoshes, and buckskin gloves twenty-four hours of each day—and when he finally discarded this outlandish indoor attire, he began a stretch of floor pacing that lasted from early morning to after midnight, and left both of his attendants with pounding headaches.

"God, that constant thump, thump, thump," Osgood complained. "And did you notice how he'd stick his nose right into the corner before turning around and heading for the opposite corner? It's a wonder there isn't a groove in the carpet. If he starts in tomorrow with the same routine, I'm staying the hell away."

But the next day Nigel went back to sitting in his armchair looking at his hands and fingers.

By that time the lunatic was alarmingly emaciated. His blue eyes were so sunken in his head, they resembled pools of pure water at the bottom of two wells. His cheeks were concave and his neck was scrawny. The tendons began to show in his forearms, and his shirt and trousers hung on his gaunt frame like rags on a scarecrow. Except for cups of cocoa, he had taken nothing into his stomach for fifteen consecutive days.

Adriana had called Providence twice, hoping to wring permission from Richard Vaughan to have a doctor come to the island and look at his brother, but on both occasions she was instructed to wait a bit longer.

"He's done this before, Miss Danziger," the politician had said brusquely. "Many times. Don't worry— when he gets sufficiently hungry, his appetite will return with a vengeance. No cause to get excited."

But the nurse knew there were other reasons for her employer's reluctance to have a stranger come in contact with Nigel. She wondered apprehensively if Richard was prepared to let his brother starve to death rather than provide him with outside help.

Still, in the end, Richard Vaughan was proven right. One Sunday evening, while Osgood was ashore, Adriana peeled an orange and placed a dish of the separated segments on the shelf inside the oak door. Attracted by the strong odor of the fruit, Nigel, who had been busy whispering to himself by the window, made a sudden dash for the saucer and devoured everything on it with apparent relish. The following day he ate all his meals, and even asked for second helpings of lamb and carrots at dinnertime. That night he sat quietly in his chair for an hour, reading a book on tapestry weaving.

When he put it aside he went to the aperture and said in a weak voice, "You can't bring the dead back, can you?"

"No, Nigel," Adriana replied, delighted to hear him speaking in a sensible manner. "No, you can't."

"Nothing brings them back. Nothing."

"I'm afraid not. Only in our memories can we make them live again."

"Yes, but memories are like dreams. They swindle you." For a moment he gaped at her, his bony triangular face behind the bars like that of a Belsen or Dachau inmate. Then he asked, "What did they do with her body, Adriana?"

"They took it away," she said, after a slight hesitation.

"Where?"

"I don't know, Nigel."

"Yes, you do," he contradicted her, but without any rancor. "You all joined forces against me—even you, my guardian angel. I can guess where she is. One needn't be Sigmund Freud to fathom the shallow mind of my wretched brother. I can guess. Supposition, Francis Bacon avowed, is greater than truth. No matter. But if you die you don't come back, and there isn't any guesswork about that, eh?"

118

"I guess not," the nurse answered.

A thin smile formed on Nigel's lips, and a sly glint kindled in his sunken eyes. "Yet it's a situation that lacks the symmetry Mother Nature usually prefers. One can change the living to the dead, but not the dead to the living. I call that unfair. Still, half-a-loaf is better than none, eh? Cain killed Abel because he was a shepherd, and Romulus slew Remus for jumping over his newly constructed wall. I have a motive for fratricide that's infinitely stronger than either."

Without another word Nigel left the door, entered his bedroom, undressed, and crawled beneath the wrinkled sheets of his cot.

From that night on he made a rapid recovery, and by the end of the week he was chatting as volubly with both the girl and Osgood as he ever had. Each morning he arose early. He even began doing setting-up exercises: running-in-place, chinning on the mantel over the door between his rooms, situps with his feet hooked beneath the armchair. In no time at all, he was a picture of health.

"I'm sure glad he straightened himself out," said Osgood one night when they were in bed. "Watching him moping around in that tweed overcoat, and listening to his whispered monologue for hours on end was really getting to me. Actually he's an interesting guy when his head's on right, funny, too. Today he was telling me about some writer—an old-time Italian—who was so poor he couldn't afford candles. So he used to do his writing by the light of his cat's eyes. That's comical, isn't it? Do you think it's possible?"

"Of course not," Adriana replied, jabbing him with her elbow. "The light in a cat's eye is only a reflection. They don't actually glow in complete darkness."

"Well, it's a good story just the same. Then he told me that shark meat will quiver for hours, even after it's been sliced into steaks."

119

The nurse grimaced. "I don't think that's funny, Ned," she remarked.

"No, but it's interesting. What makes it quiver, I wonder. Anyway, it's nice to have him acting like his old self again."

They lay silent for a while. On the night table his small radio was softly playing some Latin music.

"But I don't think he's the same man any more—not really," Adriana said finally. "I think he's undergone some subtle changes."

"What kind of changes?" the youth asked.

"Oh, changes in his manner . . . and changes in his facial expressions. To me, he just doesn't look like the old Nigel—or act like it, either. I have the feeling he's not as . . . as sincere as he used to be. Of course, I could be wrong. I may only be imagining things."

Osgood considered this, then said, "He seems okay to me, Adriana—friendlier than ever."

"Exactly, Ned. But I think he's putting it on. After all, he has no reason to be fond of us, has he?"

"You've got a suspicious nature. Why should he blame us for what happened? It was his brother who gave him the hard time."

"I don't know . . . I don't know. He's complicated. And another thing—he still whispers to himself sometimes, when nobody is around."

"He does? How do you know?"

"I caught him at it this afternoon, and he gave me a very strange look—sort of guilty and crafty and wild. Whatever you do, Edward, stay out of his reach."

"I'm not worried. I've got my stiletto. If he tries any of his cute tricks, I'll lop off his damned arm," Osgood said in an amused voice. "Besides, no matter what you say, Nigel and I are buddies. This weekend I'm going to get him an orange balloon from Holiday Park."

"How will you manage that? Are you returning early?" she asked.

120

"No, but I'll figure out a way," he answered vaguely. "Maybe I'll buy it before I go, and leave it in a locker at the bus terminal."

They talked for a few minutes more before switching the radio off and going to sleep.

· 22 ·

That Saturday morning before lunch, Nigel complained of a stomachache. Wearing his apricot-colored bathrobe, he lay on his cot clutching his belly with both hands. That he was in real discomfort was evident from the expression on his face and the worried remarks he made.

"It can't be indigestion. My alimentary system has always worked perfectly. I've never even had heartburn," he said forlornly. "I wouldn't be surprised if one of you has poisoned me."

"Nonsense," Adriana scoffed. "I'll get you an antacid tablet, and we'll see if that doesn't fix you up."

But by the time she returned from her apartment with her black bag, Nigel was in the toilet vomiting. When he came out ten minutes later, his complexion was as white as bleached parchment and he walked as if he had locomotor ataxia.

"I told you it wasn't indigestion," he croaked in bitter triumph. "Food poisoning is what it is. Some nurse you are. I suppose it's salmonella. Those wretched potatoes au gratin didn't taste right last night. Have you any antibiotics?"

He dropped back down on his bed and rolled over on his side.

"It's probably only a virus," she answered, digging a thermometer and a bottle of Emetrol from her satchel. "You know how to take your temperature, don't you? Keep it two minutes under your tongue."

"Why can't you unlock the door and come in and feel

my forehead, the way real dedicated nurses do?" he wanted to know.

"The medicine dosage is one teaspoonful every hour," she said, ignoring his request.

He dragged himself off the mattress again and collected the bottle and the thermometer from the door shelf. A few minutes later he announced in a funereal voice that his temperature was exactly ninety-nine point one.

"It can't be salmonella then, or you'd be hotter than that," she said. "Do you still have cramps?"

"I'll say I do—and diarrhea, also," Nigel replied, unscrewing the Emetrol cap. "Doesn't arsenic give you cramps? Or is it antimony? Or hellebore? Did you know they used to prescribe hellebore for crazy people years ago? It cured them, too—of living." He swallowed a spoonful of the medicine and said sarcastically, "Delicious. Where's that damned boy? Off on his furlough again? He's never around when he's needed. I really think I'm going to die, Adriana. I sense it. I have a premonition."

"You're very talkative for somebody who's about to expire," the girl said calmly. "Are your stomach pains sharp or dull?"

"Both. I'm garrulous because I'm delirious. Will you take my pulse if I stand at the door?"

"No."

"Why not?"

"I'm afraid you'll grab me, the way you did Mr. Mac-Kenzie and Edward."

"Coward," said Nigel contemptuously, as he lay back down on the cot.

Adriana opened a manual and began flipping the pages. "It could be staph," she remarked after a while.

"What?" the lunatic asked, peeking out at her from a mound of tangled bedclothes.

"I said it could be staphylococcus."

"That's a bacteria, isn't it?"

"Yes."

"Is it fatal?"

"Almost never."

"Oh, sure. Probably whole civilizations have been wiped out by it. Get that Fairoaks physician over here, why don't you? Courtland or whatever his name is."

"I can only do that, Nigel, if your brother authorizes it, and I don't think he will," said the nurse.

"Of course he won't. And why? Because he knows a doctor will be able to recognize my symptoms—be able to see that I'm dying in agony from a dose of strychnine or curare or aconite or some other damned venom. I haven't had a proper physical in three years, and even that last one was performed by a hand-picked quack who Richard felt was politically reliable. Got his license through a mail-order house in Chicago, I daresay. Perhaps I have a stomach cancer."

There were beads of perspiration on Nigel's pale brow and he looked exhausted.

"All right," said Adriana, closing the manual and dropping it in the black bag. "I'll phone Providence, and see if I can get his permission. In the meantime, you should try to sleep."

But when she got through to Richard Vaughan's mainland home, she was informed by the housekeeper that he had gone to a camp in Maine on a fishing trip, and that there was no way of reaching him there. She left a message, then called Dr. Courtland to seek his advice. The physician, after listening to her description of the illness, pronounced it a virus.

"Nothing to get alarmed about," he said with conviction. "Give him some Parapectolin and get him to rest as much as possible. Ninety percent of all gastrointestinal upsets are due to viral infection. Tell him to stay in bed, Miss Danziger. Can he follow instructions, the poor fellow? He can? Fine. Parapectolin—and if he wants anything else, give him a little sweet tea or ginger ale. Not too much, though, and no fruit juices. How's Mr. Richard

123

Vaughan these days? Keeps himself busy, I see by the newspapers. If your patient doesn't respond, if he doesn't show some signs of improvement by this time tomorrow, give me another call."

Armed with these assurances, she returned to the corridor. Nigel stopped moaning into his pillow and glared up at her. "Did you get him?" he asked.

"Your brother? No. He's away," she said. "But I spoke to Dr. Courtland, and he's almost certain you've got a virus. The worst of it should be over in twenty-four hours."

"Richard wouldn't allow me a physical examination, eh? I suppose he's afraid I'll talk about Louise. How can that damned doctor diagnose my malady without looking me over?"

"I said I couldn't reach your brother. He's in Maine, trout fishing."

"I don't believe you," the sick man declared coldly, rolling on his side to face the wall.

He spoke rarely for the rest of the afternoon. Adriana gave him what Parapectolin she had, but there wasn't much of it. When she called the pier, hoping to get Jack Flowers to bring out another bottle on his evening trip, she was informed that the boat captain was away at Mattapoag, a neighboring island, and would make his run to Scarp directly from there.

Around four o'clock Nigel finally went to sleep. Then at five-thirty the *Monica-Mae* pulled into the jetty and the nurse decided to go ashore and get the medicine herself. Leaving her patient to his fitful slumber, she hurried from the cottage, boarded the launch, and a short while later landed in Fairoaks.

The town's principal drugstore was located a short distance from the seaside at Thurston Square. It was crowded with summer visitors, however, so that fifteen minutes went by before she was waited on. At six-forty-five she left the pharmacy, crossed the street, and strolled past the little public garden in the center of the square. As she did, she noticed a young couple lying beneath some hydrangea bushes, kissing and embracing each other with considerable enthusiasm. She averted her eyes but, hearing a voice that sounded familiar as she approached the corner, she turned quickly and took a second, longer look.

The male member of the amorous pair at that moment sat up, and she was able to see his face quite clearly through the shrubbery leaves. But Edward Osgood, having eyes only for his companion on the grass beside him, did not observe the passerby out on the sidewalk.

Had the nurse been struck by lightning she could not have been more stunned. On shaking legs and with glazed-over eyes, she stepped out into the Main Street traffic. A Fiat veered sharply to avoid running her down.

Somehow she reached the pier, where she went at once to the ladies room, locked herself in a cubicle, and wept quietly for half an hour. Then, feeling only slightly better, she emerged, washed her face, and left.

An old man named Keefe, who was related to Mrs. Muldoon, agreed to take her back to Scarp in his fiberglass outboard. During the trip she spoke hardly at all and old Keefe thought she looked ill, but he didn't question her. At the jetty she offered him some money, which he refused with a wave of a gnarled hand before gunning the engine of his small craft and speeding away over the gray water.

Head bowed, the devastated girl trudged up the hill to the cottage. Nigel, who had awakened, was lying on his back and glowering at the ceiling.

"I've been calling you and calling you," he complained in a whining tone. "I feel terrible—weaker and weaker. Do you suppose I could have contracted botulism from those wretched potatoes? Botulism kills you fast, doesn't it? Unless you get a quick injection of an antitoxin made from horse serum."

Adriana replied in a lifeless voice, "Botulism is destroyed by cooking, and those potatoes came straight from the oven."

"Are you sure?"

"Yes."

Except for the murmur of his breathing, Nigel was silent for a while. Then he raised his head a couple of inches and asked, "What about cholera?"

"You're worse than a baby," she said. "Here's more Parapectolin. Take another teaspoonful and get back under the covers. I'm going down to make tea."

"Don't make any for me," the lunatic warned. "I can't stand that bilge. In any case, I'll probably be dead by the time you get back."

He got up and staggered towards the door to get the medicine.

· 23 ·

She cried herself to sleep that night, and awakened very early in the morning. Though still tired, she was too miserable to fall off again. After a half-hour's tossing about she got up and had her breakfast.

How could he have done it? she asked herself over and over. How could he have been so heartless?

There was a light rain falling, but she put on a poplin jacket and went out for a walk. Down the gravel path, through the broom-covered dunes, and along the wet dappled beach she wandered; pausing every so often to stare out at the broad and somber ocean with listless hazel eyes. Circumambulating the island at this leisurely pace, she was back in the cottage by a quarter after eight. She changed into dry clothes and then went to see Nigel.

As she entered the corridor he called to her from his bedroom, saying, "Ginger ale. More ginger ale, Adriana."

"Ginger ale?" she repeated stupidly.

"Yes, yes. That's the stuff that's curing me. I've

126

downed two bottles, and the effect is astonishing. Ginger ale. It's a magic elixir. Last night—at two in the morning, actually—I passed through the crisis. You weren't here, so I had to battle the disease quite on my own. But, with the help of ginger ale, I conquered. Get me another batch of it, though, before I suffer a relapse."

She did as he asked, bringing two bottles in from the pantry and setting them on the shelf. Nigel promptly drank a tall glass of the soda and fell sound asleep. The nurse returned to her apartment where she watched the drizzle and wept into a handful of soggy Kleenex.

By noon, however, the weather improved and the appearance of a fuzzy yellow sun high in the cloud-streaked sky made her realize that the world wasn't an entirely hopeless place. She cooked two bowls of chicken bouillon and carried them both upstairs, finding Nigel slightly less exuberant than he had been earlier, but still in a good humor. He drank the broth seated on the side of his bed, she drank hers at the desk. Afterwards she read to him for half an hour from a small blue book of Thomas Hood's poetry.

Nigel listened raptly. "He's excellent, isn't he? Just the right stuff for a convalescent," he remarked, a wistful smile on his pallid face. "Read me that couplet about the window again. Do you know the one I mean, Adriana?"

"Yes . . . yes," she said, turning pages back to locate it. "Here we are.
'I remember, I remember, the house where I was
born;
The little window where the sun came peeping
in at morn.' "

"Lovely," said the lunatic. "Not Milton or Keats, of course, but charming nonetheless. Isn't Keats a funny name, when you stop to consider it? Keats . . . Keats. Shelley's a bit quaint, too, for that matter. Keats and Shelley. Sounds like a mixed drink, doesn't it?
'Two poets were sitting out in the sun;

Robert was Browning, but John was Donne.'
Ha, ha! You've never heard that before, have you? Coup-
lets are a delight. How about:
   'An ape's an ape and a varlet's a varlet,
   Though both be clad in silk and scarlet.'
Or:
   'Up the airy mountain, down the rushy glen,
   We daren't go a-hunting for fear of little men.'
Why don't you laugh, eh? You look positively dreary—
more like Ariadne than Adriana. Ha, ha! I should think
you'd be happy, now that I've regained my health—or
almost regained it, at any rate. I hope you haven't caught
the bug from me.
   'Great wits are sure to madness near allied,
   And thin partitions do their bounds divide.'
That was written by Dryden, but I can't recall the authors
of those other gems. I really did think I had cholera last
night, because my skin felt as clammy as a lizard's. If it
weren't for that ginger ale I'd be dead by now—dead as
poor Louise."

With this final comment Nigel stretched out on the
cot, yanked the coverlet over his head, and in minutes was
gently snoring.

The nurse carried her bowl downstairs and then went
up to Grayhaven, where for two hours she helped Mrs.
Muldoon pull weeds from her small kitchen garden.

For dinner Nigel had chicken-and-rice soup, half a
baked potato with butter, and a dish of custard—all of
which he ate with a good appetite.

At eight in the evening Leon Perth telephoned. He
had spoken to the housekeeper in Providence and wanted
to know how things were going. Adriana gave him a full
report of the patient's rapid recovery.

That night, thoroughly fatigued, she slept deeply.

During the course of Monday her mood improved
somewhat. The overwhelming sense of loss that had

smothered her in misery ever since her trip to Fairoaks diminished to a point where she could now reflect on Edward Osgood's treachery without succumbing to bouts of weeping. As with all wounds, a scab had begun to form over her badly lacerated feelings.

· 24 ·

Suspecting nothing of what awaited him, Osgood disembarked Tuesday morning in high spirits. He ambled up to the cottage, rapped briskly on Adriana's door, and called her name. There was no answer from within, however, so he continued on to his own room, flung his suitcase on the bed, and carefully pushed a bulging plastic shopping bag he'd been carrying in his other hand beneath the outsized chest of drawers. After a breakfast of bacon and eggs and a hot shower, he dressed, retrieved the shopping bag, and went into the corridor.

Nigel, his face still peaked and his furry black hair more than usually disheveled, was sitting in his armchair reading an old newspaper. As soon as he saw the youth, he commenced a detailed and bathetic account of his recent illness, accompanying his remarks with many groans, sighs, and anguished grimaces. Osgood listened to him good-naturedly, now and then repressing a smile. At last the sad tale drew to a close with a stirring account of how, despite the odds, the afflicted man had miraculously managed to survive, and had even succeeded in eating a full dinner of corn chowder, roast lamb, buttered parsnips, fresh broccoli, and strawberry Jello the night before.

"But it is impossible to describe it, Edward—impossible to convey my terrors, my feelings of impending doom. To do the thing justice I would have to be a Swedenborg angel. It was said of them, you know, that

129

they were so chockful of wisdom that they could express in a single word what the wisest of men couldn't express in a thousand."

Osgood congratulated him on his recovery, then slyly opened the shopping bag at his side. From it a huge orange balloon emerged and swiftly floated up past the barred aperture. Nigel leaped from his chair as though it were in flames, dashed towards the oak door, and with his head tilted ninety degrees, ecstatically watched the rubber sphere's graceful progress along the ceiling.

"Fantastic! Magnificent! Colossal!" he exclaimed, jamming his face against the steel grill. "Oh, it's so perfect in shape and color, so dazzling, so ethereal. Look at it, Edward! It's brighter than the sun. It's the niftiest thing I've ever seen."

Laughing at the other's change in mood, Osgood pressed the button that closed the electrically operated interior door, thus separating the two sections of Nigel's domicile. Then he walked to the pantry, got the big iron key from its hook in the corner, returned, opened the oak door to the bedroom, and, with a jerk of his arm, sent the balloon sailing into the apartment.

Nigel chortled gleefully. A moment later, when the oak door was again locked and the sliding panel retracted, he flew through the archway as if propelled by rockets. As other men might embrace a voluptuous woman, the lunatic tenderly embraced the sleek orange globe. He felt it, smelled it, rubbed his cheek against it—even bestowed several loud kisses on its elastic skin.

"Thank you, Edward," he yelled happily. "You can't possibly know how much this gift means to me. It's a dream come true."

The attendant told him he was glad he liked it and, after putting the key back in the storeroom, sat in the swivel chair and lit a cigarette. "Where's my partner?" he asked.

"I haven't seen Adriana since she brought me a bowl

of porridge this morning," Nigel said, setting his new toy on the floor and releasing it. The balloon, nudged by a current of air from the window, described an elegant parabola as it rose to the ceiling. "Superb! The epitome of all that's graceful. One is reminded of Emerson's fine essay on circles. Do you suppose you could get me another?"

"Another what?"

"Another balloon."

"Someday, maybe," Osgood replied genially. "Why do you want two?"

"Because it may need company, eh? Everything should be in pairs, like the animals in Noah's ark. Do you know where Noah kept the bees, by the way?"

"No, Nigel. Where did Noah keep the bees?"

"In the archives. Ha, ha! That's quite funny, isn't it?"

"Yes—a real knee-slapper. Where do you get them all?" The youth slid his feet off the desk. "I think I'll go look for Adriana," he said.

Though he could hear the girl moving around inside, when he tried the door he found it locked. He knocked and waited. There was no response. He banged more loudly and rattled the knob. At last she opened the door, and he was shocked by her appearance. Her eyes were red and abnormally bright, her complexion blotchy. Even her curly brown hair, usually so perfectly arranged, was mussed and tangled.

"What do you want?" she inquired, lips barely moving.

"Hey! What kind of a greeting is that after four long days?" said Osgood.

"A better greeting than you deserve," she answered fiercely.

"What are you talking about? What's the matter?" he asked, startled by her behavior.

"I saw you Saturday night in Fairoaks with some

girl—that's what the matter is," she said in a voice trembling with suppressed rage.

"Me? Not me, you didn't," Osgood scoffed after the briefest hesitation. "I was in Providence ... at my mother's."

"You're a liar."

"I'm telling you, Adriana, that's where I was," he said, adopting an expression of injured innocence.

"And I'm telling you it's a damned lie," she retorted, eyes flashing. "I saw you clear as day. I heard your voice. You were rolling around on the grass in the public garden, right in the square, with this ... this cheap-looking black-haired girl in a gaudy green tunic."

"You're out of your mind. I was in Providence. Whoever you saw, it wasn't me."

"Oh, wasn't it? Then it must have been someone else—some other boy who resembled you exactly, and who talked like you and laughed like you. He was even wearing your University of Rhode Island T-shirt—the one with *Ned O.* printed on the back." She paused to catch her breath before adding, in a calmer—though colder—tone, "I may be naive and blind, Edward. I may be dense and stupid. But don't tell me I didn't see you over there the other night, because that naive, blind, dense, and stupid I'm not. Nobody could be."

This said, she slammed the door closed. Osgood, however, promptly shoved it open again. "Don't come in," she cried, blocking his path with an outstretched arm. "I don't want you in here any more. Stay out. Stay out. Stay out!"

Heedless of these hostile remarks, he grabbed her shoulder and forced her backwards, saying savagely, "Shut up, Adriana. Don't talk to me that way. Who the hell are you? I'm not your personal property. Since when do I have to answer to you for anything? You don't own me, Adriana."

"You're hurting me, Edward," the girl said, struggling to get free.

"Just because we've had a ... a relationship, that doesn't make me your goddamned slave. I don't ask you what you do when you go to Boston, do I? Then why are you so nosey about what I do on my weekends? We're not married, you know."

"And we never will be," she screamed, twisting out of his grasp and closing the door a second time. In the sudden silence the clicking of the lock was like the crack of a whip.

Osgood ran from the cottage and set off across the island with long angry strides. It was a mild day with a pleasant breeze. Out on the blue water, a dozen sailboats were heeling and sheering, jibbing and tacking. When he was as far from the nurse as he could get without leaping into the ocean, the youth sat down on a grassy hummock, lit a cigarette, and cursed his luck.

Why had she gone to Fairoaks? he asked himself resentfully. Had she been checking on him? What was wrong with women, that they had to be so possessive?

He brooded in this manner for twenty minutes, then spent another twenty scaling flat stones over the surface of the sea. Finally he went back the way he had come. As he approached the cottage he saw the bright orange balloon flying above it at the end of a length of string that extended from Nigel's living room window. Notwithstanding his black thoughts, Osgood was compelled to smile. The gleaming tethered globe cavorted about the hazy sky in fits and starts, like a fat fledgling bird.

"How did you ever get it through the bars?" he asked the lunatic, when he had climbed to the second floor.

"Patience. Little by little," said Nigel proudly. "It just made it, Edward, and naturally I was terrified it might burst, but after all these years of my gripping that steel it's as smooth as satin. You saw it from outside, eh?"

"Yes. It flies like a dream—like a soap bubble. Where did you get the string?"

"Button thread. It's strong enough, but a bit light for the job. Something heavier would give me much better control. I'm scared to death a gull or a fish hawk or osprey will take a fancy to my little aerostat and puncture a hole in it before I can haul it in. Did you know eagles are cowardly? It's true, believe it or not. Only last evening I read that the great horned owl, a far smaller bird, can actually dispossess an eagle from its nest. What was all that yelling downstairs a while ago?"

Osgood scowled. "We had an argument, Adriana and I."

"Oh? Nothing serious, I trust," said the madman, his head in the embrasure of the window and his eyes glued to the soaring balloon.

"No. She'll get over it in a day or two. Women are weird."

"Silver dishes into which we put golden apples—or so Goethe would have us believe. I knew a remarkable woman in San Jose, California, once. She could lift a wooden kitchen chair straight up, by fastening her teeth on the bottom of one of its legs. Her name was Lois Langspee. Lovely incisors, she had—and jaws like a hyena. Her husband was an airline pilot, but he never seemed to come home. With those teeth of hers she could open clams, oysters, and bottles of beer. It would do your heart good to watch her eat a bag of Brazil nuts. What was the quarrel about?"

"Nothing important," said the youth. "I don't believe a person could open an oyster with his teeth."

"Lois could. You must have quarreled about something, Edward."

"We did, Nigel, but nothing important. How old would you say Adriana is?"

The balloonist gave him a quick, cunning glance. "Around thirty, I imagine," he said.

"Thirty?" Osgood repeated in surprise. "Really? She told me she was twenty-six."

"Ah, well. Ladies often take liberties in matters of that sort."

"I figured she might be twenty-seven or twenty-eight, but I never thought she was thirty. It makes sense, though. She worked in a couple of places before she came here, and she must have been pretty old when she finished her training. I don't know why it is, but women in their thirties always go for me—and I get fooled every time. Cripes."

Nigel yanked the length of string and watched the balloon spiral downward. "Don't let it bother you," he said slyly. "When you reach thirty yourself, you won't mind it. And when you hit sixty, Edward, those thirty-year-old dowagers will seem positively alluring to you."

Osgood laughed at the remark. "You're a comical dude, Nigel," he said, "and not nearly as wacky as people think."

"At last you've hit on the truth. Better late than never. Now all you have to do, my boy, is unlock the door and I'll be on my way."

"And I will—as soon as your brother tells me to."

"My brother? Why bring him into it? He's only your employer; I'm your friend." Nigel gave the string another jerk. "But I suppose it's the old, old story—whose bread I eat, his song I sing. What if I paid you more than he does, though?"

Still smiling, Osgood studied the lunatic's face and made no reply. In his dark eyes, however, there was a glint of interest.

Nigel turned and met his gaze. "How does ten thousand dollars sound to you?" he asked.

"It sounds fine," the youth said, "but where money is concerned sound is less important than sight and touch ."

"Well, well. That's very witty," the other answered, arching his eyebrows in appreciation. "And I'd be most happy to oblige you with a look and a feel of the ten thousand, Edward, if you'll join me in a little hike up to Grayhaven—to the den behind whose fireplace mantel the money is concealed."

At these words the smile on Osgood's countenance vanished instantly. "Not today," he said in a surly tone.

"When, then?"

"Never. I'm not interested in your trick mantelpiece."

Nigel stared at him with increased concentration. "Odd," he murmured. "The last time I broached the subject, you were all ears. Do you want to remain poor and penurious for the rest of your life? That strikes me as rather silly—especially since you're not even a philosopher."

Suddenly a frightening notion entered Osgood's mind. "Has she been talking about me?" he asked suspiciously. "Adriana, I mean."

"Talking? About you? No, she hasn't. She sometimes talks about her girlfriend, Margo, in Pennsylvania, or her sister in Cambridge. But on the subject of Edward Osgood she has surprisingly little to say. Do you think that if I painted the word 'help' in large letters on the balloon, someone would come here and rescue me?"

"No, I don't."

"Neither do I. It would be different perhaps if I were a damsel in distress."

The front door of the cottage slammed. Osgood went to the hall window and saw Adriana walking up the hill with short nervous steps. "This whole place is beginning to bug me," he said irritably.

"Me, too," Nigel said, turning back to watch the graceful gyrations of the orange balloon.

· **25** ·

Furious as he had been that morning, Osgood's anger didn't last. By afternoon he was prepared to forgive Adriana her display of jealousy and forget her many nasty remarks. But, as the nurse steadfastly refused to talk to him, he had no means of informing her of his magnanimous change of heart. And for all of the rest of the week she remained aloof, too. Every day she would wander off somewhere—to pick blackberries, or read a book in a secluded spot, or help Mrs. Muldoon in the Grayhaven kitchen. Only when Osgood was not there did she visit Nigel. And if the young man entered, the young woman swiftly departed.

As for the lunatic, he observed all that happened with amused blue eyes. Now and then he would make a comment to one or the other of them, but they were not the sort of comments to bring about a reconciliation. Though neither of the combatants noticed, he was subtly stoking the fires of their quarrel.

Under these circumstances, therefore, the situation worsened. Each day's affronts by the nurse further maddened Osgood; each day's snide remarks by the youth further alienated Adriana. And Nigel, like the snake in the Garden of Eden, was cleverly deceiving both of them.

The girl caught the Friday morning launch to the mainland without uttering a word to her former lover. Osgood watched her sail away, his face contorted by rancor. In his lonely room on Saturday night he drank a bottle of California sherry, hoping thereby to dispel his bitter mood. It proved a poor idea. Glass by glass, the strong sweet wine drove him deeper into despondency.

"She has no right to treat you like this," the reasonable voice in his head pointed out. "She never even gave you a chance to explain. It's not as though that Yvonne means anything to you."

"Yvonne's all right," Osgood muttered in reply. "A nice kid. Doesn't try to slap a ball and chain on your ankle."

"Yes, but Adriana's nice too—and it's very convenient having her on the island with you."

"Not when she keeps her damned door locked," said Osgood bitterly, helping himself to some more sherry.

"Yes, that is a drag—but it can't last forever. She's bound to weaken after a while," the voice declared.

"Her? Adriana? I don't know. She's a weird chick. Got a lot of crazy ideas, like nutsy Nigel. Don't like the whole setup. I mean, that girl knows all about Louise and everything, and now she hates me. I'm in a pretty lousy position. God, why did she have to go to Fairoaks? She can get me in plenty of trouble if she starts blabbing about what she knows."

At midnight, with a muzzy head, he left the cottage and went for an unsteady walk in the open air. There was no moon, but the sky was alive with corruscating stars. Arriving at the shore, he took off his clothing and went in for a dip. The lights of Holiday Park glowed cheerfully in the distance, and he could hear the gay music of the merry-go-round over the water as clearly as if it were only a few hundred yards away.

I should go up to Grayhaven and take another look in the safe, that's what I should do, he thought as he floated languidly. If that bitch does any talking, I might have to get the hell out of here in a hurry. In that case I'll need every dollar I can lay my hands on. I should never have bothered with her. This could have been a terrific deal, but now it's turning into a disaster. I should have stayed away from her, no matter what kind of looks she gave me. Nigel said ten thousand. There was more than that in the safe, the night I was there. What's in it at this moment? I wonder. But he's right about it being illegal money, and that they can't call the cops.

He swam in and climbed the beach, intending to dress and set out for the mainhouse, but the lateness of the hour and the insidious effect of the sherry combined to sap him of all his strength. Heaving a sigh, he sat down on the shingle. Then, rolling his jeans into a pillow, he lay back on it and contemplated the awesome spectacle of the

138

milky way spanning the heavens above him from horizon to horizon. Soon, lulled by the lap of the waves on the shore, he was fast asleep.

For two hours Osgood lay there, oblivious of the world, unmindful of the universe. Over his head the great galactic wheel tilted on its axle and slowly careened to the west.

A sharp, scrabbling sound close to his ear awakened him from his deep slumber. Reluctantly opening his eyes, he discerned a vague pattern of light and shadow—it was several seconds, however, before the elements of this pattern coalesced into the form of a large black rat with a scaly tail like a length of gray cable. The bloated creature—it was as big as a tomcat—crouched less than twenty-four inches from Osgood's face, and was glaring into his eyes with feral malignancy.

Still drugged by sleep, the youth could not immediately evaluate what he was witnessing. The dark furry object reminded him of Nigel's ugly thatch of hair, and this curious association contributed to his confusion. It was not until the rat—its sinister eyes as hard and black as onyx beads, its whiskers and pointy nose quivering with inquisitive excitement—crept forward another few inches, thereby jostling the shingle and producing the scrabbling noise, that the fogginess cleared from Osgood's brain. When it did, the hair on the nape of his neck bristled and he leaped up from the ground as though impelled by a powerful subterranean current of electricity. In an instant he had climbed the bluff and was hurtling along the sinuous trail on legs shaky with panic.

Having left his sneakers and clothing behind, he experienced more than a little physical discomfort during this precipitate cross-country dash. Razor-sharp blades of dry grass, rough stones, and tough dewberry vines did their best to flay the skin from his bare feet and ankles, while sprawling thickets and the outstretched boughs of stunted oak trees and wild rose bushes whipped and jabbed his naked body with an almost human malice. Yet so terrified was he of the black beast behind him—and he was convinced it was close behind him—that he scarcely felt any of these mortifications. Fortunately, he was traveling at such a brisk speed that the journey didn't last long. In a couple of minutes he was at the cottage door, and only after he had flung it open, dived inside, and slammed it shut did he pause to catch his breath. Trembling like a heroin addict undergoing a cure, he staggered up the stairs and went to his room. On the night table his transistor radio was still playing. He did a half pirouette and collapsed on the bed, gasping for air. A moment later the sherry in his stomach commenced to bubble and churn. He fled to the toilet and was violently sick.

The following morning, nursing a fierce hangover, he collected his clothes from the seaside. There was no sign of the black rat. Uneasily, he wondered if it had been real or a product of his drunken imagination. While he was standing at the foot of the escarpment looking about, he suddenly recognized the beach. It was the one on which he had first met Louise Vaughan. With a mumbled oath, he turned and hurried away.

· 26 ·

When the nurse came back to the island that Tuesday morning, she brought Nigel two more balloons—both orange and both slightly larger than the one he had already. His joy bordered on rapture. For the next couple of days he was so occupied with flying his little squadron of lighter-than-air craft that he had little time to talk to either of his attendants. Thursday afternoon, however, seeing Adriana seated at the desk with her head in her hands and an expression of grief on her face, he moored his balloons to the window bars, went to the oak door, and said in a casual voice, "Young men are notoriously fickle."

140

She looked up at him for a while in silence, then finally remarked softly, "We were going to be married."

"Ah, that's how it was, eh?" he said, resting his pointed chin on the shelf of the opening. "When was the marriage supposed to take place?"

"After Christmas. Edward was going to finish school. He was going back in February."

"I see. Both of you would have left here."

"Yes," she admitted, nodding her head. "But now . . ."

"Now, what?"

"Now I can't bear the sight of him, Nigel. Can't stand to be in the same building with him. Can't stand his voice, the way he walks, his whole manner. The sound of his name . . . that alone is enough to cause me real physical pain." The girl bit her lip, stirred restlessly in the swivel chair, and added, "I don't understand what's happened to me. I used to be happy here, but now I'm full of fears and hatred. Why did he do it? I gave him nothing but devotion, Nigel . . . nothing but love. He became my world, my life. I adored him. I threw myself at his feet. He could have done anything to me—anything, except what he did."

The lunatic pondered these obviously heartfelt confessions, rubbing the tip of his nose against one of the steel bars. "I would have missed you awfully," he declared, blinking his blue eyes. "Love is such a paradox, isn't it? You're not the first to be mystified by it, sweet Adriana. Sappho wrote some splendid lines on the subject, twenty-five hundred years ago—about how people can love and hate simultaneously. I think it was Sappho, but perhaps it was Catullus. My memory is deteriorating, I'm afraid. It's bad when you can't tell a Greek lady from a Roman gentleman. I wouldn't have missed him, but your departure would have been a great blow."

"And I would have missed you, too," she replied.

"We've been extremely close, haven't we? For two years we've been like . . . like . . ."

"Brother and sister," he finished for her.

"Exactly . . . exactly, Nigel." The nurse brought her hands down from her temples and folded them in her lap. "But why did Edward do it? He used to complain because we couldn't have our weekends off together. Still, we were only apart for a few days. There was no need for him to chase other women, was there? I'm convinced now that he never . . . never truly loved me. His character isn't all it should be. He has weaknesses . . . flaws. I gave him fifteen hundred dollars."

"Really, Adriana? Whatever for?"

"A car. He said he had to have one."

"Fair enough, but why didn't the rogue buy one with his own money?"

"He didn't have any."

"Of course not. And why should he, if he can spend yours? That's how Richard was, when we were boys—always hanging on to his allowance, and squandering mine. I like the word 'squander,' don't you? It fits its meaning so perfectly. Have you ever heard the story of the prizefighter who retired with a million dollars, but was flat broke a year later? Somebody asked him what happened to his wealth, and he answered, 'I spent a hunnert grand on the horses, a hunnert grand on booze, a hunnert grand on women. And the rest I squandered.' Ha, ha! Isn't that beautiful?"

The girl smiled faintly.

"But I'm sorry. I didn't mean to imply there's anything funny in your situation," said the lunatic hastily. "Did Edward buy the automobile?"

"Not as far as I know," she responded in a listless tone. "He's told me he doesn't have the full amount any more—that he lent some friend six hundred dollars to pay a hospital bill."

"Do you believe him?"

142

"No, I don't. I could see in his eyes he was lying."

Nigel raised his head from the shelf and gave her a shrewd look. "Why don't you unlock this door, Adriana," he suggested, "and I'll go out to his room and break his wretched neck for you."

"No. What good would that do?"

"Well, I suppose it won't get your money back, but think of the satisfaction. Think how nice it would feel to see his silly head rolling loose on his shoulders. Haven't you ever experienced the pleasures of vengeance?"

No sooner had Nigel finished speaking than they both heard the footsteps of the youth in question approaching from the other side of the cottage. Through the door of the pantry he came, moving at his usual indolent pace.

"You haven't made lunch all week," he said, addressing the nurse in a sulky voice.

"But I did," she replied, getting up from the chair.

"Not for me, you didn't."

"No, and I don't intend to, either. Make your own. I was hired to take care of Nigel, not you."

Osgood's face grew suddenly crimson. "You always used to make it," he pointed out.

"Yes, because I wanted to. I don't want to any more," she said insolently.

"Why?"

"Because the thought of handling your food fills me with nausea."

The color of Osgood's face went from crimson to raspberry. He took a quick step forward and slapped her on the ear.

"Hey!" Nigel exclaimed.

Before Adriana could straighten up after the first blow a second and harder one landed on the other side of her head, almost knocking her down.

"You bastard!" she cried, as much in surprise as in anger. "You damned bastard!"

"Stop it!" the lunatic yelled from behind the iron grill. "Stop it, Edward!"

But Osgood's fury wasn't yet satisfied. Once more he struck the girl, this time with his hand closed. She reeled, tripped over the leg of the swivel chair, and crumpled to the floor.

"You like to talk smart, don't you?" he growled, baring his teeth. "You like giving people wise answers, but it's a mistake—a big mistake, Adriana. That's how girls get messed up. That's how girls lose their good looks. Don't smart answer me, because I'll beat your head in."

The nurse, who had been stunned for several seconds, now began to crawl backwards away from him on her hands and knees, tears welling up into her brown eyes. "You're crazy," she said huskily. "You're dangerous. A psychopath. I should have known that first night—should have realized when you killed . . ."

"Shut up!" the youth bellowed, raising his fist again and taking another stride in her direction.

"Will you kill me, too?" she asked defiantly, as a red bruise blossomed on her cheek. "Is that what you have in mind? I wouldn't if I were you, Edward. Mr. Vaughan isn't stupid—and neither is that policeman from Fairoaks."

For the next minute or two, the three of them seemed deprived of all capacity to move. Like wax figures in a chamber of horrors, they stood congealed in their dramatic poses: Nigel staring wide-eyed through the bars of his prison, Adriana cringing on the rug as tears flowed down her cheeks, and the grim wrathful Osgood with his hand clenched into a huge knot of whitened knuckles ready to strike again. Then the deathlike hush was broken by the chiming bell of the nearby buoy, and the youth lowered his arm, snarled an obscenity, turned on his heels, and walked swiftly from the corridor.

"The damned rascal!" Nigel blurted out. "How dare he do such a thing! Unlock the door, Adriana. Unlock it,

144

eh? We'll soon see whose head gets beaten in."

But the nurse, after feeling her injured face with the tips of her fingers, got up from the floor without answering him. Taking a Kleenex from a drawer in the desk, she wiped her eyes; and when she had composed herself a little, she went back down to her apartment.

· 27 ·

After the violent scene in the corridor, after being slapped and punched by Edward Osgood, Adriana harbored no more romantic illusions. The small residue of love that had lingered stubbornly in the girl's heart despite everything, at last evaporated like dew under the harsh rays of a summer sun. Fear was now the chief emotion he aroused in her breast—fear and its shadow, hatred.

On Friday the youth went ashore, however, and for the long weekend she was spared the anxiety of encountering him. Feeling freer than she had for days, she roamed the island—wading in the shallow salt ponds and rivulets, picking wild flowers and berries, watching the herring gulls and the cormorants, the scudding sailboats and the protean white clouds. Seldom did she think of her troubles—of what she was going to do—and when she did, the problem always seemed so vast and intricate that she would quickly set it aside. Like a child, she hoped some lucky event in the future might solve the dilemma for her—rectify all the wrongs by magical means.

Nigel, busy with his balloons, had surprisingly little to say about the dramatic incident in the corridor. Yet on occasion he would glance her way, and his eyes would contain a glint of understanding that she couldn't fail to recognize. For the most part he was in high spirits. In the evening after dinner he would engage in his usual haphazard chatter, relating outlandish personal adven-

145

tures and bizarre stories that he had come across in his reading. One morning, though—it was Sunday—she caught him whispering to himself in a corner of the bedroom, and when she asked him what the matter was, he only chuckled and went into the bathroom to take a shower.

It was that morning, too, that Leon Perth telephoned.

"Is Nigel all right, Adriana?" he asked in his dry, smug voice. "Has his tummyache gone? Mr. Vaughan has been concerned."

"Nigel's in perfect health," she answered. "It was just a one-day virus. He's been cured for almost two weeks."

"I'm glad to hear it. We've been away—down to Maryland to visit the chairman of the board of Jefferson-Ross Industries. They're thinking of building a plant in Central Falls. I wish you could have seen the estate that man owns. English lords don't possess grounds and buildings on such a grand and magnificent scale. I counted nine servants in the house alone. It's comforting to know that luxury and opulence are still in existence somewhere, isn't it?"

"Very," said Adriana, unimpressed. "When are you coming here?"

"Friday, I believe. It's not absolutely definite yet, because we might possibly be invited to Senator and Mrs. McLaughlin's summer home at Newport. But since the Senator's been having trouble with his gout lately, I don't expect that invitation will materialize. He spends all his time under heat lamps and in whirlpool baths, I understand. Still, it's what he gets for living on lobster thermidor and Bollinger's." The secretary giggled at his own wit before continuing. "And that's how it stands at the moment. Much as I prefer Newport, Scarp is probably where we'll end up."

"Don't you like Scarp, Leon?" the nurse asked, knowing full well what his answer would be.

146

"Don't tease me, Adriana," he said with another little laugh. "I've always detested the place—and after what happened to Louise there, my detestation has grown into a loathing that defies description. It's an odious spot, an excrescence on the face of the earth. By the way, has that grubby detective from Fairoaks been around?"

"No, he hasn't."

"Good. We were afraid he might make a nuisance of himself. Well, I guess that's everything. I'll speak to Mrs. Muldoon, so she won't be caught with an empty larder. Good-bye, Adriana."

"Good-bye, Leon."

It was only after she had hung up that the thought of complaining to Vaughan's assistant of Edward Osgood's behavior entered her mind. But what would it accomplish? she asked herself. Would they fire him? Or would they blame her for becoming involved with the young man? Whose side would they favor?

On the morning of his return, Osgood consumed his bacon and egg breakfast, took a shower, and went into the corridor with a wary expression on his face. All during the weekend he had wondered if Nigel had grasped the meaning of Adriana's angry remarks the previous Thursday. The question tantalized him. If the madman even guessed the truth, it would only be a matter of time before Richard Vaughan would learn of it, too. And that was not pleasant to think about.

"Hello, Nigel," he called to the lunatic in a friendly voice, looking through the aperture. "How are things?"

"Wretched," said Nigel, who was making cocoa at his hot plate. "I'm extremely irked with you, Edward— extremely irked. Why did you strike that poor girl? I myself have never hit a woman in my life. It's the action of a bully, a poltroon, a pimp, or a dastard. Had I been free to intercede, I would have chastised you severely."

"You're right," Osgood agreed shamefacedly.

"You're absolutely right. I don't know what came over me, Nigel. All of a sudden, I lost complete control. It's never happened to me before, I swear."

"Real men don't go around pummeling the ladies—not even in this permissive age. It was a disgusting exhibition."

"I'm going to apologize to her, and ask her forgiveness. And I apologize to you, too. I promise I'll never do anything like that again."

Nigel paused in stirring his chocolate to give him a searching glance. "I should hope so," he said sternly. "You're a member of the Vaughan family. We can't have you mistreating the fair sex like some damned French apache. Did you bring me another balloon?"

"A balloon? No, was I supposed to?" Osgood asked.

"That was my understanding. However, with all the furor, I'm not surprised that it slipped your mind. No matter. You can get me two the next time, which will give me five."

"Isn't five a lot? I mean, you're not thinking of making an airborne getaway, are you?" the youth inquired, proffering a wry grin. "We don't want you sailing off like Mary Poppins."

"Ha, ha, ha! Or Auguste Piccard. Or Monsieur Gambetta, who flew over the German lines in a gas bag during the siege of Paris," Nigel retorted with delight. "Ha, ha! No, I'm not a Montgolfier, alas. And even if I were, how far could I get, dangling from five toy balloons? Did you know that while Paris was besieged the people were so hungry they ate rats?"

"No, I didn't—and I'd just as soon not hear about it, Nigel. I hate rats, and I always have. They're the ugliest things in the world. The other night I saw one on the beach, and it scared me half to death."

"Really?" Nigel poured the cocoa into his plastic mug. "Dining habits are entirely a matter of conditioning. There's no natural reason why rats shouldn't be on our

148

bill of fare. They're perfectly good protein. I myself once ate an ear."

"Sure—an ear of corn. I've had those, too."

"No, no, no. A human ear. It was at the Willowgrove Hospital in Paxton, New Hampshire. I was there for a psychiatric evaluation, because I jumped into Lake Winnipesaukee."

"A human ear?" Osgood said, looking at him askance.

"Absolutely. The evaluation was rather comical. They kept asking me why I leaped into the lake, when I didn't know how to swim, and simply couldn't get it through their thick skulls that I wanted to commit suicide. After all, if I'd known how to swim, there wouldn't have been much point in plunging into the water, would there? A swimmer can't drown himself, even in a lake as deep as Winnipesaukee. I would say that's an excellent example of how the possession of knowledge can work to your disadvantage, eh? In any event, they hauled me back aboard my father's wretched boat before I could sink for the third and last time, and then shipped me, ranting and raving, to Willowgrove. And while I resided there I ate a human ear."

"Where did you get it, Nigel?"

"I took it off a fellow named Tyler—off the side of his head, to be precise."

"You actually ate a guy's ear? I don't believe it," said Osgood in a shocked voice. "Why would you do a horrible thing like that, for cripes sake?"

The maniac crossed to his armchair, sat down, and sipped his cocoa. "I did it for the best reason in the whole universe, my boy," he replied at last, "because I wanted to. This Tyler was a gawky lout with a mug like a mandrill's. He was crass, boorish, and incredibly stupid. Whenever I said anything, he would challenge it— virtually call me a liar. Can there be a worse combination than ignorance and skepticism? Not likely. That's a marriage formed in hell, if ever there was one. I can recall the ear episode vividly, Edward. We had just finished dinner and the subject of cannibalism arose. I offered a few tales that I had gleaned from a lurid book I had read years earlier, and this Tyler ridiculed them mercilessly. One story in particular irritated him. Come to think of it, he not only looked like a mandrill, he walked like a mandrill as well. But I suppose in a tree he would've been more graceful. It's really a pity I can't get out to a zoo once in a while. They're nifty places—in spite of the bars."

"What was the story, Nigel?" the youth asked impatiently.

"Eh? Oh, it was an incident related by a Fiji Island missionary. This savage, it seems, was standing guard over an unlucky man who was scheduled to be the main course at an impending banquet—and, feeling a trifle hungry, he ripped an ear from his prisoner's head and neatly gobbled it down, much as you or I might help ourselves to an olive from a plate of antipasto while awaiting the spaghetti."

"And this dude, Tyler—he didn't believe the story."

Nigel drank a mouthful of cocoa before answering, "No, he absolutely did not. The silly oaf maintained that a person's ear couldn't be removed so easily. Ha, ha. I brooded on his damned incivility for almost an hour; then I succumbed to the temptation of proving him wrong. His ear came loose at the first yank, though I had to give it another little tug to get it off completely."

"And . . . and you ate it, Nigel?"

"In three bites. Having gone that far, I thought I might as well go the rest of the way. Except for the lobe it was quite gristly, and none of it had any flavor to speak of. A rat would probably have been tastier. Dr. Pajalic, the director, flew into a fulminating dither—and Tyler made a fuss, too. But what could they do, really? There's no medical procedure anywhere that can restore an eaten ear, is there?"

The lunatic regarded his listener benignly, waiting

for him to comment on the anecdote, but Osgood appeared so flabbergasted by what he had heard that he could offer nothing at all.

"The palms of the hands and the soles of the feet are said to be the most delicious portions of the human body," Nigel went on, balancing the plastic mug on his kneecap. "Generally the flesh must be tough, however, because cannibals invariably sharpen their teeth to cope with it. Did you know Captain Cook was devoured by the Hawaiians? It's quite true, Edward. But at least he was killed swiftly and not roasted alive, which is how the Fijians and Papuans prepared the dish. Noble savages aren't very noble—nor are noble sophisticates, either, for that matter."

Osgood's face had lost some of its color, yet he managed to say, "Roasted them alive?"

"Yes, on red-hot stones. But there were worse practices than that. The Fiji Islanders loved to tie their captives to a tree, cut off an arm or a leg, barbecue it, and then bolt it down right before the unhappy donor's eyes. And they'd keep hacking away and cooking away and eating away until there was nothing left except gnawed bones and a few hanks of hair. Don't you find that fascinating? To devour your enemy bit by bit while he's there at the table watching you, so to speak, has to be the ultimate insult. I would have liked to have done that to my father. If you had an enemy, wouldn't you be happy to treat him in such a fashion?"

He stared up at his attendant with round inquisitive eyes. Osgood swallowed and shook his head. "That's sick," he said, wondering if the story contained a hidden threat.

"I'm reminded of a joke. Some cannibals caught a missionary, and one of them said to the chef, 'Are you going to broil him?' And the chef answered, 'No, he's a friar.' Ha, ha! Don't you think that hilarious, my boy?"

"No. I'm still thinking about those Fiji Islanders.

151

They must have been worse than wild animals."

"Of course they were. They were human beings,"
Nigel replied, grinning. "But perhaps the Congolese
were the least considerate of all. Because of the torrid
climate, their cannibals cleverly kept their victims alive
for weeks on end, while feeding off them. They would
carve the poor devils up with the greatest care, to ensure
they didn't die—knowing that live meat doesn't spoil in
even the hottest weather. Ingenious, eh? Nothing stimu-
lates man's brain, Edward, like his appetite."

A faint gurgle issued from Osgood's throat, and he
retreated from the oak door.

"Where are you off to?" the maniac called.

"I need fresh air. I'm going out," he retorted, wiping
cold sweat from his forehead and cheeks.

"Oh? Well, don't forget to come back for lunch," said
Nigel cheerily.

· 28 ·

Osgood repeatedly tried to take Adriana aside and
talk to her. The youth had concluded by now that Nigel
had missed the point of the girl's remarks the week
before—that he was still ignorant of how his wife had
died or how she had ended up in the corridor. With that
settled in his mind, his only remaining worry was the
nurse, who in her anger seemed willing to blurt out everything she knew. This to him was the worst treachery
imaginable. Hadn't she promised to keep it all a secret
that night in his bedroom? Hadn't she given her word?

One evening, seeing her descending the path from
Grayhaven with a basket in her hand, he dashed from his
room and concealed himself in her office until she had
entered the vestibule and shut the door. Then, moving
with feline grace and quickness, he blocked the way to
her apartment. When she tried to slip around him, he
caught her shoulder and gently pushed her back, saying,

"I don't want to hurt you, Adriana."

"That's a change, isn't it?" she answered tartly, though it was obvious from the small frown on her brow that she was frightened.

"I just want to talk about that Louise business," he said, displaying no emotion.

She shifted the basket from one hand to the other, and replied, "I know as much about that subject as I care to, Edward."

"Right . . . right. You know the whole thing, which is why we have a problem. I gave you that information, but you were supposed to keep it to yourself—remember? So what happens? Last week you shot your mouth off in front of Nigel, just because we had an argument."

"An argument?" she repeated, touching her cheek where the black-and-blue evidence of his brutality stood out against the general pallor of her complexion.

"An argument," he affirmed, nodding. "One that you began. But anyhow, what I'm driving at is that you have to keep quiet, Adriana. You have to stick to your promise, and not go around telling tales out of school."

"And if I don't?" she asked brazenly, ready to duck if he raised his hand.

He made no move towards her, however. Instead, he declared in a voice as hard and sharp as the cutting edge of an axe, "If you don't, there'll be trouble—and most of it will be yours. What you got upstairs is nothing compared to what you could get. When a man and a woman are alone—in a room or a car, or on a quiet beach—there isn't much the woman can do to protect herself. You see what I mean? She's pretty well defenseless." He paused, then smiled and continued in a lighter tone. "Come on, Adriana, use your head for once. All the evidence is gone. It's at the bottom of the ocean, miles from here. Nothing you say will make any difference in the long run, because nothing can be proved against me. I'm in the clear. The law can't touch me any more."

153

The nurse licked her lips, transferred the basket back to the other hand, and said, "Mr. Vaughan doesn't bother much with the law, Edward. From what I've seen lately—from what we've both seen—he likes to make his own laws."

Osgood shrugged. "Uncle Richard doesn't scare me. If you told him what you know, he probably wouldn't even believe you—and if he did, what the hell could he do? Richard Vaughan has a lot more to worry about than I do. I mean, if a little rumor can ruin the guy, how can he afford to give me a hard time? You heard Leon. They're paranoid on the subject of publicity."

"In that case," she said, "why is it so important for me to keep silent?"

"Because I don't want any trouble," Osgood answered, his voice becoming sharp again. "Not even a tiny bit."

Instinctively she stepped backward, interposing the basket between them. "I don't want any trouble, either," she said, the words rushing from her mouth.

"Good. Then we understand each other."

"But I want you to return my money."

Once more he smiled. "That's something we'll have to see about, Adriana. A lot will depend on how you act," he said.

"All right," she agreed, not looking at him, "I won't reveal your secrets to Mr. Vaughan or the police, but you have to stay away from me, Edward."

"Okay—no problem. You keep your mouth shut, and I won't go near you," he said jovially. "Of course if you don't, the situation could change."

"Will you let me by, now?" she asked in a subdued voice.

"Sure, go ahead."

She sidled past him, trotted down the hall, unlocked the door to her apartment after some fumbling, and disappeared inside.

Edward Osgood, manifestly pleased by what he had accomplished, went out for a stroll.

· 29 ·

"I'm not flying my balloons today—the wind is all wrong," said Nigel, gazing through his opera glasses at the sea. "I let them out this morning for a little exercise, and they sailed up and over the cottage. I couldn't even see them, Adriana. And then, when I reeled them in, I was terrified that the rough edges of the roof tiles would rip them to shreds. But I was patient and careful, and now the darlings are resting safe and sound beneath my bed. Isn't it wearing to have responsibilities? Oh, there's a cormorant—just beyond the jetty. The first time I saw a cormorant I thought it was a sea monster, because it was black and so much of its body was under the water."

"I'm going to leave, Nigel," the girl said.

"So soon? You just got here?"

"I mean I'm going to leave Scarp—go back to Boston."

"Really?" he asked, lowering the glasses. "Why?"

"I . . . I can't stay on here . . . with Edward."

"Well, have him fired then. I won't miss the rogue. Tell my brother it was he who killed Louise, and I'm sure your problem will be solved very nicely." He watched her from the corners of his eyes. "How did the murder happen, by the way?"

Until that moment, Adriana—like Osgood—could only guess at the extent of the lunatic's knowledge. She had hoped he hadn't understood the significance of her threats and accusations that day, but now she realized Nigel had understood every word. Leaning against the oak door, she sighed. "I can't talk about that," she said.

"Why not?" he inquired. "We're all in on the secret together, aren't we?"

"I've promised not to discuss it with anyone."

155

"A promise to a scamp like Edward is worthless. Are you afraid of that boy?"

"Yes," she confessed. "And with reason." The nurse bent her head. "I never wished I was a man before, but I do now. If I were, I'd soon teach him a lesson. I'd beat him up—punch him, the way he punched me. Only I'm not a man—and Edward is vicious . . . a savage."

"Too true," Nigel said. Then he resumed looking out of the window. "The cormorant is an entertaining creature. Whenever they dive beneath the surface, I try to guess where they'll reappear. But the ocean is so vast, I don't think I've ever been right. If you let me handle young Osgood, figuratively and literally, he won't trouble you any more."

Adriana laughed—a brittle sound, like the cackle of an old woman. "I believe it," she acknowledged. "You'd kill him."

"Oh? Why in heaven's name should I want to go that far?"

"Because of Louise."

"A life for a life, eh? His death wouldn't resurrect the poor girl, though, would it?"

"No, it wouldn't. Still, you'd kill him in revenge," she stated flatly, raising her head to watch him through the bars.

Nigel chuckled. "That, I admit, is a seductive idea. The whole wide world comprises nothing sweeter than sweet revenge," he said with feeling. "But, there is revenge and there is revenge. Murdering an enemy isn't always the cruelest punishment you can inflict on him. I myself consider death a rather overrated form of chastisement—unless, of course, it's administered in some ingenious manner. Crucifixion isn't bad, though impaling is probably better. And there's a lot to be said for skinning alive, too. However, refinements of this sort are impracticable, nowadays." He began polishing the lenses of his opera glasses with a handkerchief. "In Edward's

156

case I wouldn't gain a thing by murdering him—aside from the pleasure, I mean. Richard would throw another fit, and I'm certain I'd never survive a second dose of that damned screeching radio. By the way, is he definitely coming this weekend?"

"Mrs. Muldoon says they'll be here Friday afternoon," the girl responded. "Are you worried? I'm sure he won't bother you."

The lunatic answered with a short, enigmatic laugh. "Did you know the people of the Hebrides eat cormorants?" he asked. "It's a fact. They boil them in oatmeal. I wonder what Dr. Johnson thought of that. Not much, I imagine. And the Roman soldiers lived on oats during campaigns, just like horses. Their staple diet, it was. The Saxons, on the other hand, concocted a kind of booze from honey and oatmeal, which must have been a real eye-opener." He slipped the binoculars in his pocket and left the window. "Listen to me, Adriana. I give you my solemn word not to do Edward any permanent injury, if you let me out of here for an hour or so. And you know I'll abide by that oath. I've never once lied to you on an important matter, have I? If I make a serious pledge, I honor it—and fastidiously."

"I couldn't release you, Nigel. It would be like releasing a lion from its cage," the nurse said gravely.

"Nonsense. A lion? What a fanciful idea! I've done a few wicked deeds, yes—but only when I've been in a manic state, when the balance of my mind has been upset by severe and prolonged provocation. This would be an entirely different situation. I'd be as cool and deliberate as a glacier. Isn't it true, Adriana, that ordinarily I'm a very reasonable person? Isn't it true that I'm usually quite calm? If it weren't, how would I have lasted ten years in these concrete cubicles? Remember, too, I once escaped from here—the time I worked the pins out of the hinges with the coat hanger—and I didn't behave like a wild beast then, did I? I didn't hurt a soul."

"But Mr. MacKenzie told me you fought them desperately—that they had to tie you up with clothesline."

Nigel shrugged. "Naturally, I resisted. I wasn't anxious to be imprisoned again," he replied blandly.

"And you won't be anxious this time, either," she said. "No, I can't. I wouldn't even dare open the door, for fear of what you might do to me. Who can guess how you'd act? And I'd be responsible. I could get into very bad trouble."

"You exaggerate. Let's suppose that this Friday morning, just before you catch the launch to go home for your long weekend, you come up here and leave that ugly wrought-iron key on the desk. And let us further suppose that after you've gone I procure the key, and a little later in the day when Edward Osgood comes slouching in, I give the wretch the thrashing of his life."

"And then?"

"And then I return to my quarters, lock myself in, and toss the key back on the desk. If I could, I'd even hang it on the hook in the pantry for you, but that, alas, is impossible."

Nigel crossed to his armchair and glanced from beneath drooping eyelids at the girl, estimating the effect of his argument.

Staring vacantly into space, she said, "I don't believe you'd voluntarily go back to jail. I don't believe it."

"Well, you should. It makes sense, doesn't it? What have I to gain by not going back, eh? Can I escape? How? I can't fly like my beloved balloons, can I? And I can't swim. And those damned dinghies in the shed are all chained together like rosary beads, so they're no help. Furthermore, I'm swearing to you on my sacred honor that I will return to my cell. Yet you can't accept my word. Why? Am I a fraud, a prevaricator, a humbug, a hypocrite? Really, Adriana, you're not being fair to me." The lunatic circled the coffee table and wandered several steps in her direction. "Bear in mind, also, that I'll be doing you an inestimable service, because as long as that young thug goes unpunished you'll be at his mercy. And he's amoral, a murderer, perhaps even a sadist. In time he'll terrorize you into submission. In fact, he might kill you because of what you know. But, Adriana, if you permit me to take some of the starch out of him, to box his ears a bit, believe me, you'll have nothing further to fear. On earth there's no tamer brute than a whipped mongrel. And once he's chastised, things will return to normal, eh? You'll be able to remain here on good old Scarp, and you won't have to worry and fret any more."

They both became silent. Out on the sea a boat passed by, and carefree shouts drifted in the corridor windows. There was laughter and, for a moment, the lilt of a female voice singing a popular tune.

Suddenly, Adriana began to cry. Huge tears like opals tumbled down her cheeks, and her shoulders shook convulsively with every sob. "I'm miserable," she said in a choked voice, "miserable and afraid."

Without haste, Nigel ambled to the door. "Ah, Adriana, don't weep. There's nothing to be afraid of," he declared gently. "I'll take care of everything."

"I can't do it . . . I can't," she murmured, moisture sparkling on her eyelashes like raindrops on a spider's web. "It would be too dangerous, Nigel."

"Dangerous? How? If I promise not to injure Edward, which I do, and if I swear to return to my apartment afterwards and lock myself in, which I do also, what have you to fear? You know I'm not really a monster—a raving maniac. If it weren't for the vile persecutions of my father and my brother, I'd be living a normal life this very moment."

Reaching through the bars, Nigel placed his hand on her brown curly hair and patted it. Adriana opened her eyes, and found his face a scant six inches from her own.

"Do you know," he said tenderly, "this is the first

time I've ever touched you. In all these months that we've been together, I've never felt your hair or the smoothness of your skin."

The girl ceased her sobbing. "I . . . I'll have to think about . . . about what you've been saying," she stammered, backing slowly away.

"Yes, of course. But there's not a lot you'd have to do." His hand left her head and came to rest on her shoulder, which he grasped lightly. "Just leave the key there—make a mistake, faultless Adriana. And I'll manage that Edward Osgood for you."

She retreated another step. He made no effort to detain her. The tips of his long fingers slid the length of her bare arm almost to the wrist. "I'll have to think about it," she repeated weakly, contemplating him with glistening puzzled eyes.

"I ask no more than that," he said, withdrawing his hand inside the door. "Thoughts are the seeds of future deeds, as someone has cleverly noted."

Then he went back to the window, took out his opera glasses, and resumed watching the cormorant.

· 30 ·

The weather became increasingly hot and muggy. So saturated with moisture was the atmosphere that moving through it was like wading in lukewarm water up to the eyes. Osgood went around in shorts, drank iced drinks, sat in front of his electric fan, went swimming and took frequent cold showers, but nothing seemed to help. The air was just too thick and viscous, and the temperature too high.

"Why doesn't Uncle Richard buy a couple of air conditioners?" he asked Nigel peevishly on Thursday afternoon. "Nobody uses fans these days. They went out with bow ties and short haircuts."

"Usually the island's quite temperate, even when it's

160

sweltering elsewhere," said Nigel, who didn't seem at all bothered by the heat. "I can't remember its ever being so warm and sticky."

"Maybe, but I notice there are air conditioners up at Grayhaven," Osgood answered morosely, "and they're not being used, either. Meanwhile, we're sweating like pigs in this damned steam bath. Christ, I wouldn't mind if I could go someplace at night—someplace temperature controlled, like a movie—only there's no way. Last weekend I went to Falmouth, Mass. We ate in a restaurant where the thermostat must have been set at sixty-five. I wish I was there now, though. Ever been to Falmouth, Nigel?"

The lunatic, occupied with shining a pair of shoes, answered, "Yes, many years ago. Don't remember much about it, however."

"Me and this girl went there on a bike."

"A bicycle?"

"No, no. A Honda motorcycle. I borrowed it from one of the dudes in Fairoaks, and Yvonne and I just took off for three days. We had a super-cool time. The only thing that spoiled it was Yvonne's mother, who raised holy hell when I brought her back Monday. There are still a lot of people living in the dark ages, I guess. God, to hear that woman talk you would have thought I kidnapped the girl."

Nigel daubed black polish on the edge of one shoe's sole. The sharp smell of the substance filled the air. "I've been on a motorcycle," he remarked, a trace of pride in his voice.

"There's nothing like it in the world," said Osgood, smirking. "It's a really beautiful sensation, especially with me, because when I get on a bike I fly. Nobody passes me. I make them all swallow my exhaust."

"The motorcycle ride I had occurred in California," Nigel declared, a twinkle in his eye, "and it was a rather upsetting experience."

161

"In what way?"

"I was hitch-hiking. I had just escaped from an asylum called Rose Hill Manor, you see, and had succeeded in reaching the highway outside Sacramento, but no one would pick me up. Not that I could blame them. It was after midnight, and I suppose I appeared a rather wild character in my white duck trousers and my tennis sneakers. Still, eventually I did get a lift, from a bearded fellow on a motorcycle, and I was extremely grateful for it, too. So, off we went in a tremendous roar with the wind whistling about our ears. It was a chilly night and I was uncomfortable, but I felt such ecstasy at getting away that I bore my discomfort willingly."

"What kind of a bike was it?" Osgood asked, watching him with an amused expression on his face.

"I have no idea, but it made a terrible noise. When he started up, I thought my eardrums would burst like bubbles. There was only a single seat—a long leather saddle, theoretically meant to accommodate two people—and no handholds of any kind. I was obliged to wrap my arms around the waist of the driver. And since I hadn't any goggles, I crouched down behind him to escape the fierce wind. There we were then, a couple of frail creatures shooting along the highway like homunculi astride a bullet from an express rifle, the night around us as black as the bottom of Lake Avernus—which the Romans say is the entrance to hell—and only a wavering shaft of golden light from the thing's small headlamp to guide us on our journey."

Nigel, shoe in one hand and brush in the other, paused and looked dreamily towards the barred window, as though able to see again that road from Sacramento, three thousand miles beyond the western horizon, and himself and the other man tearing along it on the thundering vehicle. "How fast were we going?" he asked rhetorically, as he resumed applying boot polish. "Seventy miles an hour? Eighty? I don't know, but at every bend in that highway, Edward, the three of us—pilot, passenger, and machine—were compelled to lean over at a forty-five-degree angle, and this caused the sky above us to tilt as though the whole universe had fallen off its rails. Nevertheless, being relatively young at the time, I was rather enjoying this mad headlong voyage through the gloom—until I became aware of a most disquieting circumstance. The motorcycle, I need hardly tell you, was vibrating like a jackhammer, and this wretched vibration was inexorably bouncing me further and further back on the seat. To prevent that from happening I gripped my companion more tightly, but this did me no good at all since he too was being jiggled in the same direction. What distressed me, you see, was that when I first got on the monster I never noticed if there was a fender covering the rear wheel. And now, unable to communicate with the bearded chap because of the infernal racket, unable to let go of him with one hand in order to explore the afterpart of the damned boneshaker, and unable even to turn far enough around to get a glimpse of what lay behind, I was in a state of considerable trepidation. Ha, ha! You can appreciate the awkwardness of my position—eh, Edward? I was riding a tiger, so to speak. In a matter of minutes I was bound to be forced off that jouncing saddle—and, when that happened, on what would I land?"

The youth grinned broadly through the barred aperture, and said, "I see what you mean, Nigel. You were pretty well convinced you were going to sit on a spinning rear wheel. That would've made anybody a little anxious."

"Ha, ha! Well put. A little anxious. Ha, ha! And so things stood. Or sat, to be more precise. Millimeter by millimeter my backside was retreating, taking me along with it. At the very end of the saddle there was a slight incline—a lip designed to follow the contours of the human anatomy—and I devoutly hoped that this would be enough to keep me where I was until the driver had to stop for a light, or a tank of gas, or a cup of coffee. But the raised edge only slowed my retrogression. It failed to bring it to a halt. Like a thing with a mind of its own, my rump climbed up the lip and teetered there for what seemed a lifetime. Ah, Edward—the poignant thoughts that passed through my head! Unless a man has experienced such an ordeal, such a trial by fire, he can never really understand the nature of desperation, desolation, and dismay. While I perched there on that thin leather rim, though it couldn't have been for more than a minute or two, my brain positively teemed with vivid philosophical insights. I knew with absolute certainty the difference between the material and the spiritual, between good and evil, between subjective idealism and objective idealism, between heaven and hell, between justice and injustice. And it was all so self-evident and simple. In the entire cosmos there were actually only two valid propositions—the first, that my behind should stay on the seat, and the second, that it should not. The former was right, the latter wrong. Ha, ha! Never before nor since have I so fully grasped the true meaning of reality.

"But, alas and alack, the greatest concentration of mental activity by the finest mind on earth isn't sufficient by itself to change in the least degree the direction taken by a speck of dust dancing in a sunbeam. The motorcycle hit one last bump on that winding road, and the faithless saddle slipped out from under me. Down I plunged."

Nigel stopped, smiled benignly, and began diligently working polish into the gaps between the lace holes.

"So what happened?" Osgood asked impatiently.

"What happened?" the other repeated. "Why, nothing. The wheel, I discovered to my joy, was covered by a broad, solid fender that was every bit as comfortable as the seat. On it I finished the journey to San Francisco without further incident."

Osgood seemed disappointed. "You were lucky," he

164

said. "Suppose there hadn't been a fender. What would you have done then?"

The lunatic considered the question solemnly for a moment, before answering, "I guess I would have become a soprano."

"Right," said the youth, nodding and chuckling.

"I would have become a soprano and sung in the opera. Ha, ha, ha! Wouldn't that have been nifty? A single revolution of that wheel, had it been uncovered, would have altered me completely. Ha, ha! Just think of how well I might have performed the mad scene in *Lucia di Lammermoor*. Ha, ha, ha! And I've never ridden a motorcycle since, which gives you some idea of the size of the scar it left on my psyche. But better there than elsewhere, eh?"

Nigel roared gleefully, waving the dauber like a wand, and Osgood, infected by his mirth, was soon laughing along with him. By the time their fit of hilarity ebbed, both had aching sides and tears in their eyes.

· 31 ·

Prior to boarding the *Monica-Mae* for her trip to Fairoaks Friday morning, Adriana went up to the second floor and sat at the desk in the passageway. Nigel, though awake and listening, remained in bed and pretended to be sound asleep. For five minutes the nurse lingered there, with only the occasional creak of the swivel chair to betray her presence. Then, as softly as she had come, she departed.

Nigel counted to fifty under his breath, threw his long legs over the side of the cot, and got up. He padded barefoot to the door and peered through the grill. In the center of the green blotter on the desk lay the ornate key.

"Ah-h!" he sighed. Wrinkles of gladness furrowed his face, and his eyes shone. "Perhaps there is power in prayer," he murmured. "Perhaps there really is a righteous God."

Turning, he went to his clothes closet, and from it obtained three stiff paper tubes, each nearly a yard in length. These he fitted together by inserting the tapered ends into the tapered openings, and when he was done he had a seven-foot stick that resembled an oversized billiard cue. To the tip of this instrument he attached a short piece of string equipped with four wire hooks made from bent safety pins. He then hastened to the living room, thrust his improvised fishing pole through the bars of the door, and in a surprisingly brief time snagged the key by its baroque oval bow. As soon as he had the wrought-iron device in his hand, he commenced a silent though sprightly dance around the coffee table—a dance that seemed to borrow its steps from both the lindy-hop and the saltarello. A moment later, however, he resumed his labors.

Since there was no keyhole on his side of the oak door, he tied the key at a right angle to a section of the papier mâché tube, and after a good deal of poking and jiggling he managed to stick it in the lock from the outside. Next he jabbed the end of the narrowest tube through the filigreed handle, and by dint of some acrobatic contortions was eventually able to rotate the key the necessary 180 degrees, and thus to hear the gratifying click of the bolt sliding free of its mortise.

Very deliberately, so as to savor the experience, Nigel pushed open the door, stepped over the sill, and filled his lungs with air. Grinning like a hobgoblin, he shoved his hands deep in his pants pockets and strutted up and down the corridor, halting every so often to perform more pantomime capers on the rug, and to make low sweeping bows to an invisible audience.

Then, after a quick peek into the pantry and a look in the desk drawers, he returned reluctantly to his apartment, locked the door again, and deftly retrieved the iron key. The cough of Flowers' diesel engine reached his ears as he was hiding this precious object behind some paperbacks in his bookcase. He ran to the window. Beneath him and perhaps a hundred yards away the launch was slowly moving out from the jetty, its prow cleaving the glassy surface of the water like a surgeon's scalpel carving flesh. On the deck, wearing rose-tinted circular spectacles and dressed in an immaculate white halter and a jonquil-yellow skirt, stood Adriana Danziger. He blew her a kiss, but she didn't see him.

It was close to eleven o'clock before Osgood came on duty. Far from leaping from his prison to assault the young man, Nigel greeted him affably, and for the next two hours entertained him with a seemingly inexhaustible stream of lively chatter. He told him of how the water shrew was such a ferocious little animal that it would kill a fish sixty times its size, by biting its eyes out. And of how the conquistador Cortes built his ships of mahogany. And of how it took fifty-eight seconds for a lobster to die in boiling water. And of how Jonathan Swift's brain exceeded 2000 cubic centimeters in volume, but Anatole France's was barely half as large. And of how Thackeray said he liked first-rate wine and second-rate women. And of how dots weren't put over the letter "i" until the eleventh century. And of how a cremated man of average build is reduced to slightly less than four quarts of ashes.

Snatches of poetry, amusing anecdotes, and even a few dirty jokes were included in this monologue, and Osgood, sprawled in the swivel chair with a cigarette in one hand and a tall tumbler of iced coffee in the other, snickered, giggled, and guffawed in rollicking good humor at everything he heard.

At one o'clock the youth left to have his lunch, however, and, except for a brief visit late in the afternoon, Nigel didn't see him again until dinner time.

Shortly after six, while he was finishing the last of his meal, the lunatic heard the motor launch returning to the island, and he went again to the window. There on the jetty was Osgood, waiting to lend a helping hand to Richard Vaughan—resplendent in a tennis shirt and Bermuda shorts—as he came ashore. Perth, attired in his usual business suit and carrying a briefcase, followed his master up the gangplank, a vaguely disgruntled expression on his small face.

"Lovely," Nigel whispered. "The mountain has come to Mahomet."

· 32 ·

Osgood sat up in bed and tried with a brain still dimmed by slumber to recollect what it was that had awakened him. The fan in the window droned on monotonously with all the dull perseverance of a garrulous after-dinner speaker, yet somehow the air in the room stayed leadenly stagnant.

Had there been a clap of thunder? he asked himself. Was a storm brewing finally?

He lit the lamp and with blinking eyes glanced around. Everything seemed in order. Perhaps he had only been dreaming, and had awoke for some reason now buried again in the depths of his unconscious.

But, as he turned his pillow over and prepared to flick off the light, a soft scurrying sound came from the hall outside, bringing to his drowsy features a look of puzzled anxiety. Into his mind leaped a vision of the black rat on the beach, and a tingle of fear traversed his body. The time, he saw, was five past two in the morning.

Much against his inclination, he got up, struggled into his blue jeans and sneakers, and went to the door. He opened it cautiously, peered out—and beheld nothing. With a groping hand he located the light switch on the wall and clicked it on, flooding the landing and the stairs in a yellow glow. No bloated rats were skulking there, but he did notice that the door on the far side of the pantry was partially closed. Grumbling to himself about ventilation and air circulation, he shuffled down the hall, entered the storeroom, and shoved the offending portal back against the wall, fixing it in that position with a can of fruit salad from one of the shelves. As he straightened up, he saw that Nigel's living room door was standing slightly ajar.

"Christ!" he muttered, his eyes starting from his head.

The fear that assailed him earlier, when he had heard the soft scurrying noise, resurged in him now multiplied by a factor of ten. His heart lurched and the saliva in his mouth became as tacky as mucilage. The warm pantry suddenly grew as cool as an icehouse.

Yet for all his fright, he realized he would have to investigate this sinister circumstance. There was no way of ignoring it. Osgood took a step into the corridor and listened, hoping to hear the sonorous breathing of the sleeping Nigel, but he heard only the faint slap and clatter of the tireless sea waves on the distant shingle. He crept forward and looked through the opening into the bedroom. The cot was empty, and the man who usually occupied it was nowhere in sight. Dashing to the second oak door, the youth stared desperately into the living room. That, too, was vacant. Nigel had escaped. He was out roaming around.

"Son-of-a-bitch!" Osgood whispered, aghast.

Shaking his head in bewilderment, he turned the corridor lights on and ran to the desk, where he snatched up the receiver of the telephone—but, even before his ear told him the instrument was dead, his eye perceived the mangled end of the wire resting on the carpet a foot from its baseboard terminal. He dropped the phone on the desk. It struck the top with a hollow crack, and at that precise moment all the lights went out, plunging the place instantly into total gloom.

The nape of Osgood's neck prickled unpleasantly, while his legs became as untrustworthy as those of an invalid. Nevertheless, he wasted no time in fleeing back to his bedroom, though it cost him some hard knocks on his shins as he passed blindly through the cluttered pantry.

Once in his own quarters again, he bolted the door and sat down trembling. The sudden darkness had unnerved him more than anything else. His own lamp was now off, but light from the jetty filtered in the windows—enough of it to enable him to see the gray outlines of his furniture.

"The bastard's thrown the master switch . . . in the cellar," he murmured indignantly. "There's no juice in the whole cottage."

Osgood, having caught his breath, went to the huge armoire and from a bottom corner took an almost full bottle of sherry, which he uncapped and raised to his lips. After two long quaffs, he wiped his mouth on his bare forearm and said, "How the hell could he do it? How could he get the key? Or did he pick the lock somehow?"

With the bottle in his hand the youth began pacing the bedroom, unanswerable questions jostling each other in his excited brain. Several times he halted, put his ear to the door and listened for any activity without, but no sound whatever could he detect.

Probably gone down to the boats, he thought. Probably trying to hacksaw that chain, or smash it with a hammer and chisel. There are plenty of tools in the basement.

The notion of Nigel with a hammer in his hand caused his stomach to flutter. He helped himself to a third swig of sherry.

Now that the electric fan was no longer working, the small room grew hotter and hotter. Sweat poured from Osgood's body. It stung his eyes, trickled along his naked spine, dripped from under his arms. From the top of the chest of drawers he picked up his horn-handled knife, snapped it open, and stood for a while contemplating its slender tapered blade. Then he set the bottle on the bedside table, went to his kitchenette, and procured a flashlight from the cabinet there.

"This should get me to Grayhaven," he declared in a confident voice. "And once Uncle Richard and I team up, the crazy son-of-a-bitch is as good as back in his cage."

At that point he remembered his portable radio, which was sitting on the nightstand, and a crafty smile parted his face. He took it, strode to the door, and went back out on the landing. The cottage continued to be eerily silent. Osgood pressed the button on his flashlight and was gratified to see a cone of brassy light radiate from its broad lens. He then turned the transistor on, tuned to a program of jangling modern jazz, and boosted the volume to its limit. The herky-jerk gasps and squeals of a tenor saxophone, accompanied by some energetic percussion work, annihilated the stillness in an instant. With this shield and the torch in his left hand, and the open knife in his right, he started down the stairs.

There was no one in the vestibule. Shooting the flashlight's beam into Adriana's office and the rear hall, he scanned all the recesses and corners, but he saw no sign of the escapee. The cellar door, he noted, was closed and bolted.

By now the sherry wine had fortified his resolution. He felt brave, tough, indomitable. Preceded by the cone of light and surrounded by the radio's clamor, he crossed the foyer, threw open the front door, and stepped onto the gravel path. Up out of the darkness a foot came. It struck his right wrist, sending the knife flying off into the shadows. Osgood had time enough to whip the torch around, and time enough to recognize the madman's grinning face in its bright ray, before a powerful blow to the jaw knocked him over backwards. Stupefied by the punch, he was a minute or two regaining his senses, but by then his attacker was seated firmly astride his chest, and had pinned his arms to the ground with a pair of bony knees. When the last wisp of fog cleared from the youth's brain, it was too late to do anything except squirm and tremble. The switchblade was resting lightly on his throat, and an iron hand gripped his head by the hair. Above him Nigel, wearing the earphones, glared triumphantly like a surrealistic apparition.

"Ah, Edward," he said in a gloating voice that overrode the spasmodic jazz coming from the radio, which was now somewhere in the shrubbery. "Ah, Edward—I've got you at last. You, the fulsome little brute who murdered my poor, sweet, gentle Louise. Did you really think I would let you get away with it? Did you think those bars and those panels of oak would protect you forever? Ah, Edward! How stupid you are! You thought you had an angel by the finger, but you had the devil by his claw."

Osgood made an effort to speak. His vocal organs, however, had petrified with terror and no words came forth. He dared not try to free himself, dared not even move, lest the maniac apply more—and fatal—pressure on the dagger at his throat. At length he heard a voice in his ears, and discovered to his surprise that it was his own.

"N-no . . . no. I had n-nothing to do with it, Nigel," this unfamiliar quavering squawk was protesting. "I . . . I d—didn't touch her. How could I, Nigel? I didn't even know her. It was . . . was your brother. Yes, Nigel. He did it. He killed her. I only helped Leon put . . . put . . . put her body in the trunk. That's all—I swear."

While Osgood was delivering his desperate plea the lunatic went on grinning and glaring, his milky blue eyes beneath their drooping lids like shards of Delft porcelain. Suddenly the youth realized that his words weren't being heard, that the earphones completely prevented him from communicating with the man who at any moment might end his life. He groaned in despair.

"A bad night's work, that was," Nigel remarked, giving his captive's hair a malicious tug. "Murdering my dear wife, Edward, was an ill-considered enterprise. Murdering my beautiful Chloe, my little Juliet, was rash in the extreme. But how shall I compensate you for your

172

treachery, eh? Shall I pluck out your eyes? Slit your throat? Disembowel you? Extract your miserable black heart? Pull out your lying tongue? Shall I slice off your ears and nose, and make a meal of them? Shall I chop off your arm and roast it in Adriana's oven, like a loin of pork? Shall I flay you and fillet you, Edward? Ha, ha! But all these penalties seem so tame and lenient—hardly more than slaps on the wrist. To do the job properly, to punish you as you deserve, I would have to be a Caligula or Tamerlane or Vlad the Impaler. Ah, Edward! How inadequate I feel! Still, I have your fancy knife with its fancy horn handle, eh? A fair amount of mischief can be done with that, I'm sure. Did you know that the caribou is unique among deer in that both sexes have antlers? No? You don't read enough, my boy. However, pleasant as it's been, we must part. Farewell, Edward, farewell."

Through a film of tears Osgood saw Nigel raise his arm. On his hand, which was closed into a fist, he wore a tight buckskin glove. Osgood began to whimper. Then the fist descended like a meteor falling from the inky sky. His brain wobbled in his skull, and he observed nothing more.

The smell of fuel oil and moldy earth was what he became aware of first. He opened his eyes. An almost perfect darkness met his abstracted gaze.

Where was he? What had happened? Why did he feel so tired? Why wasn't there any light? These questions and others crossed his mind in an erratic procession. He rolled onto his back and sat up. Why did his head hurt? And his jaw? Where was he?

Slowly, like someone assembling a jigsaw puzzle, he began to remember. He'd gotten out of bed. There was a noise. He'd gone into the corridor. Nigel wasn't in his cot. Nigel had escaped. And then all the rest of the story drifted into his consciousness and he shivered with fear.

But as his mind gradually cleared, his apprehension

173

lessened. The mere fact that he was still alive was a lucky break—one he had never expected when he was pinned beneath the taunting madman on the gravel path. How long ago was that? he wondered.

Using a hard horizontal surface—a box of some kind—as a support, he struggled to his feet. At once he recognized that he was in the cottage cellar, more by the odor of the place than by any feature he could discern. Arms extended, he started to move cautiously forward, and after two steps touched a rough stone wall. He turned to his right and soon encountered an iron garden seat, an outdoor grill, a carton of croquet balls and mallets, and finally the oil heater. With this last object as his polestar, he was able to calculate where the staircase was. A minute or so later he found and mounted it. And when he tried the door, to his surprise and joy, it opened easily.

Bright light blinded him, but his eyes adjusted swiftly and he saw that the source of this brilliance was the articulated lamp on Adriana's desk. After looking right and left, he ran into the nurse's office and armed himself with a heavy bronze bookend. The desk clock revealed the time to be a quarter past three. He must have been unconscious for nearly an hour, he realized in astonishment. Touching his tender jaw with the tips of his fingers, he stared at the small dial in disbelief. But if it's that late, he reflected, the sun will be rising in a couple of hours. He had better get back in his room, lock the door, and wait until then before attempting to get help from Grayhaven.

Leaving the office, he switched on the hall light and stealthily climbed the stairs. The landing was empty. He paused there and listened, and a strange sound reached his ears. It was the measured buzz of somebody snoring.

Could it be? he asked himself, leaning exhausted against the newel-post. Had the crazy bastard actually gone back to bed? What had happened? Had he tried to get a boat free, failed, and decided the hell with it? With a nut-case, anything was possible.

Osgood began to feel giddy. His door stood half-open and he longed to go in and lie down and sleep. But at the same time, he fully appreciated that he would sleep a great deal more soundly if he knew Nigel was once again safely under lock and key.

Bolstered by this argument, he tiptoed into the pantry. There the snoring was louder and unmistakable. He entered the corridor and peeped through the bedroom grill. Nigel, evidently dead to the world, was stretched out on his cot, the expression on his face one of infantile innocence. Osgood quietly tried the oak door. It was locked, as was the living room door when he tested that a moment later.

"God!" he whispered.

He crept to the desk, softly pulled open a drawer, and saw his headset lying within. The telephone then caught his attention, and he followed its brown cord with his eyes. The once-loose end was now reconnected to the terminal box.

"For chrissake!" he muttered. "Did I dream it all?"

Groggy as he had been, his discoveries rendered him more so. An enormous weariness engulfed him. He had to get to bed. That was the only thing that mattered. He had to rest . . . sleep. In the morning he would tackle these mysteries. In the morning he would question Nigel, and call Uncle Richard. In the morning . . . in the morning.

Like a zombie he made his way back to his room and kicked off his sneakers. The lamp was again lit on the nightstand, and beneath it was his radio and the flashlight.

"Tomorrow," he said, under his breath. "I'll worry about it tomorrow."

He removed his blue jeans, flung them on a chair, went into the bathroom, and turned on the fluorescent light.

What he saw sent him reeling backwards. On the walls and shower curtains, in the tub, on the tile floor, on the mirror, in the basin, and on the top of the hamper, there was blood—glistening scarlet smears of it. Osgood's mouth fell open in amazement. He put his hand to his forehead. The blood was everywhere. It was like some gruesome exercise in finger painting, done by an insane child. Even the cover of the toilet had been dabbed, decorated with red blobs that could have been crude geraniums.

On the hook by the sink a bloody denim shirt hung, and on the rack a bloody white towel was draped. There were two bloody sneakers on the floor, a bloody glove and a bloody pair of pants nearby.

Catching a glimpse of himself in the mirror, he was horrified to see that there was blood on his face, too, and, when he held up his right hand, that also was stained a vivid crimson.

"I must've got it from . . . from the doorknob . . . or the switch," he said in a tone that was vague with wonder. "What . . . what is it? What the hell does it all mean?"

It was then that he heard the growl of an approaching motor boat. Stumbling from the bathroom, he went to the window that faced the sea, parted the dimity curtains, and saw by the floodlight's broad glow a blue launch putting into the jetty. Emblazoned on its wheelhouse was the yellow insignia of the Fairoaks Police Department.

Osgood's heart quailed in his breast.

· 33 ·

Adriana, her face as white and lifeless as sculptured alabaster, was met at the bus terminal by Raymond Calderone, and together they set off on foot for the police station.

"Did you see Osgood before you left yesterday morning, Miss Danziger?" the detective asked.

"No, I didn't," she answered, struggling to get her thoughts in order despite the spasms of horror and fear

176

that were tormenting her mind. "He was still sleeping, I guess—and Mr. Vaughan and Leon Perth hadn't arrived yet. It's very strange. I'd half-forgotten they were coming out this weekend."

"Did you have any reason to suspect there'd be trouble?"

"None," she said quickly, almost brusquely.

But Calderone took no notice. He appeared sallower than ever in the sunlight, and there were dark blotches beneath his pink-bordered eyes. "The kid must've gone berserk," he said. "There was liquor on his breath. Liquor has a funny effect on some guys. What about arguments . . . tensions? Was there anything like that going on?"

They walked by a group of teenagers gathered in front of a pizza parlor, and she used that as an excuse to delay her reply, while she wondered anxiously where his questions would lead her in the end. Then she said, "Edward and I had several quarrels recently. We . . . we had a close relationship until about three weeks ago, when we broke up because I discovered he was seeing another girl."

"And there were hard feelings," he stated flatly.

"Yes, though the last few days we got along fairly well. Not that we were friends again."

They threaded their way through the slow-moving Main Street traffic. As they reached the sidewalk, Calderone said, "You were close, huh? I'm sorry I have to dig into your personal life, Miss Danziger, but were you sleeping with this guy?"

"Yes," she responded in a voice that was nearly lost in the noisy hum around them.

"What kind of fellow was he? You're a professional nurse. Was he a stable type, would you say—or was he quick to fly off the handle?"

"He was impulsive . . . and willful."

"Uh-huh. Did he have a temper?"

"At times."

"And a tendency to be violent?"

Adriana lowered her eyes. "Edward . . . Edward was inclined to treat people roughly—yes," she said, with apparent reluctance.

The detective gave her an oblique glance. "Did he ever push you around?"

"Yes."

"Ever hit you, Miss Danziger?" he persisted.

"One day he did. He struck me three times—two hard slaps and a punch that knocked me down," she answered, bitter and ashamed.

Four gaudily dressed tourists, their grinning faces sunburnt to a salmon red, approached them. Calderone waited till they passed before saying, "I'm sorry to hear that—sorry, but not surprised. Did you know Osgood was a convicted felon?"

"No . . . no," she stammered, plainly taken aback. "Was he?"

"Yeah. He beat up his ex-girlfriend and swiped her automobile—but she went to the police and he was arrested and tried. The judge let him off with probation, and after that the girl's tires kept getting slashed wherever she parked. Then one night when she was driving home alone from a dance, somebody heaved a brick through her windshield from an overpass. She was lucky, though. Only got a couple of scars from the glass. Nice, huh? The Providence police tried to nail Osgood for the crime, but they didn't have any proof. I got this information last month, after I came back from Scarp. What could I do with it, though? I knew the kid was Vaughan's relative, and I didn't want to stick my neck out. Now two people are dead."

He ran his hand over his crew-cut gray hair and scowled at a Toyota that was standing much too near a fire hydrant.

They turned a corner and the sea came into view. A bank of haze obscured the dark profile of the island, however. Only a faint smudge indicated where it lay. Adriana stared at the smudge, her mouth grim and slightly puckered.

"Have you at any time seen Edward Osgood with a weapon, Miss Danziger?" her companion asked.

"He owned a knife—a switchblade," she said. "It had a handle made out of antler. He used to sharpen it on a whetstone, and keep it oiled." She took her eyes from the distant shadow in the bay, and for the first time looked directly at Calderone. "But . . . but couldn't the murders have been committed by a prowler? Men do sometimes land on Scarp at night and steal things," she declared hopefully. "Mr. Muldoon lost a portable electric generator from his greenhouse that way."

"No," said the detective, shaking his head emphatically. "We've got the kid cold. At 2:50 this morning, Richard Vaughan called us and told the sergeant at the desk that Osgood had just attacked his secretary with a hunting knife, and was at that moment banging on his locked bedroom door and threatening to get him, too. Vaughan was scared silly—almost hysterical. But, of course, we couldn't get out there in time to give him any help. What happened afterwards, we figure, was that Osgood smashed a window, climbed in, and stabbed his boss about a dozen times. He must've been in a frenzy. The room was a shambles."

The nurse, though she maintained a stony expression, was startled by this revelation. How could they be so sure it was Richard who telephoned? she wondered. The policeman on duty would not have been familiar with his voice.

"They got me up at three o'clock—I had an hour's sleep, only—and we raced over there as fast as we could push the launch, but, like I say, it wasn't fast enough," Calderone continued. "Vaughan and Perth were both dead. I don't want to give you a lot of gory details, but it was pretty bad out there—about as bad as I've ever seen."

"I can't believe it. It's too . . . too savage," Adriana said plaintively. "I can't . . . can't believe it."

"That's how it is with homicides," he replied in a sympathetic tone. "Nobody ever expects sudden death. They figure it can happen to other people, yeah—but not to a friend or a relative or to themselves. Anyway, the old lady and the old man—the Muldoons—they were okay. The two of them slept right through, and didn't hear a sound. That's the kind of ears they got." His sallow face registered astonishment. "We ran down to the cottage. Osgood met us at the front door and started telling us a wild story, but he didn't have too much to say when we found his bloody clothes in the bathroom. Actually he was pretty groggy from the liquor he had. Could hardly keep his eyes open. Of course, he'd been in a fight, too, and had a couple of black-and-blue marks on his jaw, which can also tire a man out. Vaughan was a big guy, and I'm sure he didn't die without putting up a battle."

"But why would Edward do it?" she asked. "He always seemed to like his uncle. Why would he hurt him?"

Calderone ducked his head to avoid some low-hanging rhododendron branches. "According to our reconstruction of the crime," he said, "the kid went up to Grayhaven to steal money, and Perth caught him in the act. You see, there's a safe behind a movable mantelpiece in Vaughan's office there, and Osgood knew about it. We noticed it because he was in such a hurry, he didn't shut it all the way. Also, he left some blood on the wall. In his room under his box-spring, we found $3500 dollars taped to a bed slat. The knife was on top of his wardrobe. He hadn't even bothered to try to clean it."

Taking her arm, the detective guided her down a side street. "We'll have to go through this parking lot and use the back entrance, Miss Danziger, because there are reporters in the lobby. Would you believe there are guys up here from Washington, D.C., already? If the weather were

180

clearer you could see a whole fleet of boats out there, going round and round the island. Some of them have TV cameras on them, too. Well, it'll be good for the local business people, I suppose. Personally, though, rubber-necking ghouls always turn my stomach."

To the girl, the red-brick slate-roofed police station appeared forbidding. They had arrived too fast, she felt. She wished they could walk some more—past the pier or out towards Holiday Park.

The interior of the place was as murky as a cavern. At the end of a narrow hall, two men were standing next to a water-cooler. With a start, she recognized one of them as Nigel Vaughan.

"Adriana! Adriana!" the lunatic called to her excitedly. "It's so good to see you. Have they told you? Have you heard the incredible news? My brother's dead . . . and poor Leon Perth, too. Edward killed them—for money, they say. Can you imagine? Why would he do that, Adriana? I didn't know he needed money, did you? Wasn't he well paid? He did it with that push-button knife of his—stabbed them in the middle of the night at Grayhaven. Isn't it rather thrilling? Like acting in *Macbeth* or *Titus Andronicus* or something. Are you glad to see me? Still alive? Ha, ha!"

"Yes, yes. I am, Nigel," she responded guardedly, gazing into his blue eyes as if to fathom the workings of his mind.

"I'll leave you here a minute, Miss Danziger," said Calderone. "I got to go find an office that isn't being used."

"Three o'clock in the morning," Nigel blurted out, as the detective vanished through a doorway. "That's when it happened. Isn't it noisy here in town at this time of year? I had no idea the cars made such a dreadful racket. There was blood everywhere, Adriana. We used to have a gardener, back during the Second World War—his name was Tiller, believe it or not—who claimed that hydrangeas loved blood. He said it was the only plant food that really made them flourish. He'd get the stuff by the bucket from an abattoir in Pawtucket. Bucket from Pawtucket. That's an unconscious rhyme, isn't it? The whole business is positively staggering. I never dreamed he had a murderous disposition. Edward, I mean—not Tiller, who must have gone to his ancestors a decade ago, at least. Did you anticipate such a horrendous tragedy, Adriana?"

"No, I didn't," the nurse answered, giving him a hard look. "If I had suspected anything like this was going to happen, I . . ."

"But how could you suspect it, eh?" he broke in on her, a mischievous twinkle in his eyes. "He seemed so young and innocent—a mere lad, with the down still on his cheeks. Of course, he did have that bizarre fantasy of conquering the world like Alexander the Great, but most of us have our delusions, don't we? Even if you had been there, you couldn't have done much—and it might have been dangerous for you. It's just as well you suspected nothing."

The plainclothesman, who all this while had been ogling the girl, now said in an amiable voice, "Aren't you going to introduce me to your friend, Nigel?"

"Oh, I beg your pardon," the maniac apologized. "This is Albert Macy, Adriana. And Albert, this is Adriana Danziger. Albert and another policeman have been chaperoning me." He made a small gesture with his right hand, and she noticed for the first time that the two men were handcuffed together. "It was weird walking down to the jetty—strange to tread on grass and stones instead of that wall-to-wall broadloom. Almost eleven years I dwelt there—more than a decennium or two lustrums or half-a-score. Aren't the blueberries huge this summer?"

"How do you do?" Albert Macy said. "Haven't we met somewhere before, Adriana?"

"I don't believe so," she said, certain they were total strangers.

182

"Didn't you use to go to the Luna Disco out on Jenkins Point?"

"No. I've never been there in my life."

"Funny. I guess there must be another girl in this town that looks just like you," said the plainclothesman, a husky individual with modishly styled hair and a Viking moustache.

Nigel smirked. "Then she has a double, eh?" he said slyly. "I thought I'd be seasick on the boat, but I wasn't. They're sending me to Parkstone. Will you visit me there, Adriana? You and I—we're the only ones left. We'd better stick together, eh? Otherwise, things could get worse than they are already."

"Yes, I'll visit you," she agreed, though there was little warmth in her voice.

"But now that I see you closer," said Albert Macy, flashing a devilish smile, "it suddenly strikes me I'm wrong. That girl at the Luna ain't half as pretty as you are."

"Oh, oh! Watch it, Adriana," Nigel exclaimed in mock alarm. "I think this young man has something on his mind. Ha, ha. Even in a police station, Cupid twangs his tiny bow."

The nurse blushed, but nonetheless maintained her poise. "He's too kind," she murmured, bestowing the briefest of glances on the Fairoaks Lothario.

Somewhere in the building there was a clanging sound, as of a gate being slammed shut. Nigel grinned at her foolishly. His furry hair was plastered down on his head with water or hair tonic, and he had evidently made an attempt to part it on one side. He said, "But that Edward—what an evil person he turned out to be! Shame on him! We're lucky to have survived, aren't we? I guess it only goes to show you have to be careful nowadays—eh, Adriana? Careful, careful, careful, careful. Careful what you do, careful what you say. One mistake and it's curtains, as the gangsters used to snarl. One wretched, petty, paltry slip and you go sailing off to limbo like a thing on wires."

To Adriana these last remarks of the lunatic were so obviously a warning that she couldn't imagine the plainclothesman missing their meaning, but when she furtively looked in his direction she found Albert Macy too busy surveying her bosom to take notice of any subtleties in his prisoner's conversation.

"Naw," Albert declared, his Viking moustache quivering with restrained desire. "She doesn't have the figure you got, Miss Danziger—not by a long shot. She's nice and all, but she just ain't in your class. Maybe some night me and you can go out to the Luna, if you're going to be around. I'm on days the whole week. They got a cool group playing there—from England, like the Beatles. What do you say?"

"I'm sorry," she answered, shaking her head. "Under the circumstances, I don't feel much like dancing. But thanks for the invitation."

"Oh. Sure, I understand," he said, disappointed. Then, to show that he wasn't vanquished yet, he radiated his roguish smile. "Maybe another time, huh? This is a small town, so I'm sure we'll be meeting here and there."

"Ah, Albert—you're a smooth operator," Nigel remarked with a leer. "Smooth as silk. But beware—one of your colleagues might have to arrest you for stealing hearts, and you'll land in jail. Ha, ha. Did you know Cardinal Richelieu had an enemy of his locked up for sixty years? Sixty! In a dungeon of the Bastille on a lettre de cachet. And prisons are such depressing places. No offense, Albert. Wasn't that vicious of the Cardinal? Wasn't it, Adriana? How would you like to spend a lifetime behind bars? Or even half a lifetime? You wouldn't, I'm sure—and I don't blame you. But they did give me a nifty lunch here. More than ample portions, too. Collops of baked ham, and dollops of mashed potatoes. And there were two desserts: ice cream and a Granny

Smith apple. It was nice dining out, for a change. Well, I'm relieved to know everything is going to be all right again. There are more ways to kill a dog than by choking him with butter, eh? I only wish Albert would invite me to the Luna Disco. I wouldn't refuse. Ha, ha. I'd go in a minute. Yes, I'd raise Cain, if I were able—though I wouldn't raise Abel, if I were Cain."

The madman grinned, frowned, blinked owlishly, then grinned again.

A woman wearing bifocal spectacles stuck her head out of a doorway to the right of the water-cooler and called, "Dr. Farnum is here, Albert."

"Okay. That's us, Nigel. Let's go," the plainclothes-man said, taking a last fleeting look at his new acquaintance. "So long, Adriana. Nice meeting you. I'll see you sometime, huh?"

She nodded.

"Yes, yes. Good-bye, Adriana. Farewell," Nigel exclaimed, suddenly agitated. "You will visit me soon, won't you? Please? Don't wait too long, eh? And take care, take care. Don't think me ungrateful. Take care, my sweet Adriana. I wish you nothing but happiness."

The nurse waved to him, her expression a blend of uncertainty and sorrow. The door shut and she was alone.

She waited a few more minutes in the gloomy hall, picking nervously at the strap of her shoulder bag, and then Calderone reappeared and escorted her to a cramped office with an ancient rust-cankered metal desk and a battery of old-fashioned wooden file cabinets. Atop one of the latter a small fan was frenziedly trying to circulate the stale heavy air.

He motioned her to a chair covered with a plastic cushion, sat down himself behind the desk, and remarked mildly, "You people kept telling me Nigel was an idiot when I was out to Scarp—but he isn't, is he?"

"He has his good days and bad days," she replied noncommittally.

"Don't we all? Still, I doubt if even on his bad days he's as simpleminded as you folks claimed he was. Why was everybody so cozy, Miss Danziger?"

She folded her hands in her lap, closed her eyes wearily, opened them after a few seconds, and answered, "Mr. Vaughan believed having a psychotic brother was a political liability. He insisted we pretend to the outside world that Nigel was only retarded—mentally deficient—because he felt people sympathize more readily with that than with insanity."

"He didn't miss many tricks, did he?" the detective said wryly. He drew his black notebook from the pocket of his jacket and dropped it on the desk. "The reason I'm asking about Nigel is because Edward Osgood is giving us his version of what happened out there, and in it your psychotic patient is supposed to be the killer."

Though she had known it was coming, the blunt statement sent a shock wave of apprehension to the pit of her stomach. "Nigel?" she said. "How could Nigel be involved?"

"Yeah, that's the question," Calderone retorted, leaning back in his chair and tapping his chin with the end of the ball-point pen. Behind him a large iridescent housefly was frantically trying to burrow its way through a corner of the dingy-paned window. Its drone was loud and full of fury. "According to the kid, he woke up in the middle of the night and found one of the barred doors open. And Nigel had flown the coop. So he went to look for him, but Nigel ambushed him in the dark and knocked him out cold. That's how he got a hold of the knife, you see. Osgood says he came to in the cellar, and when he ran back upstairs he discovered Nigel had returned to his little prison and was sleeping like a baby, with both doors securely locked again. Then he went to his own room and there was blood all over the place. What do you think, Miss Danziger?"

"I don't know," she said in a feeble voice. From her

186

bag she pulled a handkerchief and patted her cheeks and temples. "Do you think you could raise that window a little, please? It's stifling in here."

"Sure." He hopped out of the chair and complied with her request. "The point is, could Nigel have escaped?"

"He did once, by unfastening the door hinges. However, they changed the hinges after that, and the new ones couldn't be taken apart," she declared, breathing deeply of the cool fresh air that billowed into the office.

The iridescent fly buzzed off into the sunshine, and Calderone settled back in his chair. "It was a pretty peculiar arrangement out there, wasn't it? For ten years Vaughan kept his brother under lock and key—behind steel bars, in fact—and nobody knew about it. There are laws against false imprisonment, but I guess they didn't worry him. I don't want to get into that, though. Anyhow, the kid claims Nigel managed to open the door, yet my experts say the lock is a Chinese puzzle that even Houdini couldn't pick—certainly not from the inside. There's no pick marks, either. And the key is a barrel key, hollow at the tip, which means it fits over a stubby pin in the lock—and that pin is what makes it so tough to monkey with. We figure he could only get out of there if he had an accomplice—but who would help him? The Muldoons? The victims? You weren't there."

The detective studied her for a moment, his close-set eyes converging to give him an eerie cyclopean appearance. "Osgood says that Nigel, after locking him in the basement, went to his room and dressed in some of his clothing," he resumed unhurriedly. "Then he ran up to the mainhouse, committed the two murders, came back, planted the money and the bloody knife, dumped the clothes in the bathroom, and took a shower. All very efficient, for a lunatic. Next, he unbolted the cellar door so the kid would be free to shoulder the blame, returned to his own apartment, locked himself in as magically as he had let himself out, and jumped into bed." Calderone paused again, and again gave her a searching look. "And that, Miss Danziger, is Osgood's story."

Adriana wiped her lips with the handkerchief. "Could . . . could it have happened that way?" she asked.

"Sure, if Nigel was able to escape. But how could he, huh? And there's also the matter of the telephone call. We haven't told him about that yet. We'll spring it on him this afternoon, maybe. It might be just the thing to break him down."

"Were there fingerprints?"

"At the scene of the crime? No, he wore gloves. They were in his bathroom with the rest of the stuff. We don't need fingerprints, though, because we have plenty of evidence. This is an ironclad case. Osgood hasn't a prayer. If he's smart, he'll plead. The D.A. might be willing to settle for second degree. I think he planned to frame Nigel, to pin it on him in some convincing way, but we got out to the island too fast for him. You know something? He's even claiming Nigel killed his wife, Louise, and that Richard Vaughan had a couple of guys stick her in a trunk and drop her in the ocean. When I was over to Scarp that time I told him about a fisherman seeing a cabin cruiser around there the night she drowned, and I'll be damned if he didn't work that into his story, too. Why would Vaughan want to cover up for his crazy brother? It don't make sense. But Osgood's got a great imagination—better than those people who write for the TV."

Adriana pressed the handkerchief to the side of her mouth, and said, "It's too incredible . . . too fantastic."

"Yeah, but it's real enough for us," he replied impassively. "We practically caught the guy red-handed. If ever there was an open-and-shut case, this is it. He even left one of his cigarette butts in Perth's bedroom, when he was ransacking it. He must've been crocked. But it's lucky for us there aren't any mysteries or complications, because Richard Vaughan had a lot of friends in this

188

state—heavyweights, important people. The switchboard's been tied up since seven this morning. So we got to handle this thing perfectly, or they'll be calling for special commissions up in Providence to investigate it like a political assassination. Already we're getting outside help that nobody here asked for. How about a cup of coffee, Miss Danziger? Or a Pepsi?"

"Yes . . . coffee, I think," she said.

For an hour the detective kept her there, going over virtually all that had happened on Scarp since Osgood's arrival at the beginning of the summer. He patiently inquired about the youth's general behavior—his opinions, how he got along with his employer, his attitude towards Perth, whether he ever did any pilfering, how often he drank and how much, and whether he took drugs or smoked pot, how he treated Nigel, and so on. It was a painful experience for the girl, yet she managed to answer the questions concisely and with few hesitations, while he scribbled in his black notebook.

At the end of the hour they left the office, went up a flight of narrow stairs, and entered another small room. There, on a glass-covered desk, eight switchblade knives were neatly arrayed, each with a numbered tag. When asked if she recognized any of them, she promptly identified number six as the one Osgood had carried about with him on the island. A uniformed policeman then typed a short statement in which the knife was described in minute detail and she signed it.

After that, Calderone led her out into the hall again and toward the rear of the building. In front of a green, sheet-metaled door he stopped and said, "Osgood has asked to see you, Miss Danziger. Do you have any objections?"

She gave him a quick, distrustful glance. "I'd rather not," she said weakly.

"Why?"

"Because I'm frightened."

"Of what? He can't hurt you. He's locked up, and I'll be right beside you. The fact is he's been raising a rumpus, insisting that he's being framed—and that you're the one person who can prove his innocence. To get him to shut up, I told him you'd drop by for a few minutes." The detective smiled, revealing some widely spaced front teeth. "Come on," he said encouragingly. "There's nothing to worry about."

With that he opened the door and ushered her into a large room that contained four cells, only one of which was occupied. The tenant was Edward Osgood. His face was misshapen by a swollen jaw, and there was a yellow-blue welt on his right cheek. But the dullness and lack of animation in his dark eyes altered his aspect even more than did his injuries. He appeared haunted. His cambric shirt was half-unbuttoned, and there were no laces in his sneakers.

As soon as he saw her, he said, "What did you do, Adriana? Did you help him? You unlocked his door, didn't you? Or gave him some kind of tools so he could unlock it himself. You'll have to admit it, now. They're blaming me, Adriana. For chrissake, tell them the truth. Tell the whole story. You wanted to get back at me for slapping you, right? You were pretty sore about it, so you let Nigel loose to cause me trouble."

The nurse, clutching the strap of her shoulder bag in both hands, licked her lower lip with the tip of her tongue and said distinctly, "No, Edward, I didn't do anything like that. I wasn't even there."

"But the plan went wrong, didn't it?" the youth continued, as though she had never spoken. "The bastard tricked you. Nigel outfoxed you. For a month he's been scheming, thinking of revenge. He got hold of my knife, Adriana, and went up there and killed the two of them. Then he left the bloody clothes in my bathroom to make it look like I did the murders. You never expected that, did you? So, tell them. Tell them. They'll understand. It was a mistake, right? You didn't figure he'd kill anybody. He tricked you. Tell them. God! You're an honest person, Adriana, not a liar. Admit what happened. Tell the cops what you did."

She met his dull stare without wavering. "I didn't do anything," she answered firmly. "I don't know what you're talking about. I was away in Cambridge."

Osgood ran his hand through his bushy hair and sighed profoundly. He raised his black eyes momentarily to the ceiling, brought them down again to her face, and said laboriously, "It's the only explanation that fits. The only one. He's not a magician. You must've helped him—given him the key or something. And Nigel had the moves all worked out. Don't you see, Adriana? Now they'll ship him to an asylum, and the first chance he gets he'll take off like a bird. That was the whole idea. And he's dangerous. A murderer. So you have to tell them, because you're a decent human being. You have to tell the truth."

"But I've told the truth, Edward."

"You haven't, you stinking bitch!" he suddenly shrieked. "You haven't, or I wouldn't still be in here. You haven't the guts to tell them. You helped that bastard, and now you're afraid because he killed the both of them. You bitch! You're his accomplice. Admit it!"

"Hey! Take it easy, boy," Calderone said severely. "You got to behave, you know. Otherwise we'll have to stick you someplace a lot less comfortable. Watch your mouth in front of the lady."

"Should we go?" the girl murmured, tugging nervously on the leather strap of her bag.

"No, no. Don't go yet," said Osgood, instantly penitent. "I won't yell any more, I promise. I'm sorry I got mad, Adriana, but this is a real scary situation. I mean, it's serious. They want to put me away for twenty or thirty years, and I'll never be able to take that. I'll crack up . . . get soft . . . commit suicide. That's why you have to help me, Adriana. You have to remember how close we were. That other girl—she never meant anything to me. Strictly a casual acquaintance, I swear. So look," his voice grew gentler and more persuasive, "you tell them about how Nigel strangled Louise, and how Uncle Richard went in there with the radio, and how her body was stuffed in the trunk and those two dudes came out from the mainland and dumped it in the ocean. Just tell them that. I've tried to and they don't believe me. But they'll believe you. Tell them, Adriana."

She gazed at him: at his frightened face and slumping shoulders, at his open shirt, his tanned arms, his slightly twitching hands, his beltless jeans. He seemed a stranger—a different man from the one she had known and adored. "Louise Vaughan drowned," she declared, in an uncompromising tone, "and her body was never recovered."

"You lie!" he snarled, gripping the bars as if to tear them from their sockets.

"Come on, huh? Behave yourself," Calderone barked. "I did you a favor bringing Miss Danziger here. And now you're insulting her. Is that any way to act?"

"I'm sorry, Adriana," the youth said hastily. "I don't know what's the matter with me. I didn't mean that. I'm sorry about everything. I'm sorry . . . sorry . . . I swear. But you're not going to let them lock me up for a thing I didn't do, are you? And they might even bring back the death penalty in this state, a guy was saying this morning. You don't want me to die just because we had an argument, do you?"

The nurse shook her head and bit her lip. "I don't want you to die, Edward, but there's nothing I can do for you," she replied.

"Osgood, you were supposed to provide me with a lot of fresh information if I brought the lady to see you," Calderone said, scowling angrily. "You promised to be more cooperative. So what have you given me? Nothing,

192

that's what. You're still babbling the same old nonsense. Your story is full of holes, boy. Even if Miss Danziger gave Nigel the key—and I don't believe that for a minute—it doesn't solve your problem. When we got there the key was in the pantry—on a nail in a corner behind the door, wasn't it? And Nigel was locked in his apartment, right? Okay, then. If he locked his door with that key, how the hell did he get it back on the hook in the storeroom there? It's a physical impossibility, no matter how many paper tubes and pieces of string he had."

"I know . . . I know," the man in the cell answered. "He must've had a tool—a screwdriver or something like that. What did you give him, Adriana? A piece of wire? A pair of thin pliers? Some strip of metal he could . . . But don't go. No. Wait. Don't go without telling what you gave Nigel. Please, Adriana."

The girl had started for the door, however, and when she reached it she flung it open and fled into the hall.

A minute later, Calderone joined her. She was standing by a barred window, sobbing quietly.

· 34 ·

The dark green sea scrambled up the beach, fanned out into a pool of blinking froth upon the sand, and then reluctantly receded. Adriana let her eyes wander slowly over all the familiar features of the small crescent cove— the gnomish spruce tree, the tawny bluffs crowned with broom and heather, the flat stone that had so often served as their picnic table, the wild rose bush, the pit where they built their fires, the cleft in the rocks where they cooled their wine. It seemed impossible that only a few weeks had gone by since their last little party at this snug and private place, impossible that everything was over between her and Edward.

"Why did it happen?" she asked softly.

At the tip of the crescent's southern cusp two plovers

strutted on spindly yellow legs along the shore, their sun-bleached beige bodies almost invisible against the background of sand.

"Why did it happen?" she repeated, a note of anger in her voice.

Around the narrow headland an outboard motorboat sped, trailing a lacy wake like a bridal train. The roar of its engine startled her, while the plovers immediately flapped their wings and flew up into the sky, showing their black-spotted tails and whistling plaintively.

Turning, she went back the way she had come. The sun was bright, yet she felt oddly chilled. "He never loved me. Not really," she murmured. "He lied . . . and he cheated. He never loved me. Never."

At the jetty she was surprised to see Raymond Calderone, chatting with Flowers and Coombs. When he spied her approaching he left them abruptly, however, and hurried forward.

"How are things, Miss Danziger? Got all your belongings packed, huh?" he said, smiling and showing his widely spaced teeth.

"Yes," she answered. "I'm ready to leave."

"It's been a rough deal for you, but you'll get another job easy enough. And after awhile you won't remember much of what occurred here." He took her arm and led her away from the small pier. "Tell me something," he said, lowering his voice. "Was there a second key?"

"To Nigel's quarters? Yes, there was," she responded, having decided the previous day that this was the safest reply she could make to that particular question.

"Who had it?" he asked.

"Richard Vaughan, though I have no idea where he kept it. I never had occasion to use his key."

Calderone's sallow face registered mild annoyance. "It could have been anywhere, then—even in Providence?"

194

"I suppose so. Why? Is it important?" she inquired, pretending ignorance.

He shrugged and said, "Not really. It's just that Osgood has dreamed up a new theory, and I have to check it out—otherwise some cagey lawyer might clobber me at the trial. On the witness stand you have to be ready with all the answers. What the kid suggests now is this: Nigel got the regular key from you and used it to escape—and when he returned, he locked himself back in with the second key, having taken it from his dead brother. You see the point, Miss Danziger? If this was true, it would explain how the original key was still hanging on its hook in the pantry. What do you think, huh?"

"How could Nigel be sure he was going to get the second key?"

"Maybe he knew where it was kept, up there at Grayhaven."

She looked doubtful. "Did you find this other key in Nigel's apartment?" she asked.

It seemed a long while before he answered. She waited, scarcely breathing. At last he said, "No, it isn't there—and that's where the theory comes apart at the seams. We turned the place upside down—dismantled the furniture, tore his mattress apart—and found nothing. We even went over the ground outside his windows, square foot by square foot. A complete waste of time. So if the guy had that extra key, what did he do with it? If he tried to flush it down the toilet, it would've got stuck in the trap. We checked the trap. It wasn't in there. And before we took Nigel to the launch that day, we searched him thoroughly, which means he couldn't have thrown the thing in the ocean when nobody was looking." Calderone grinned again, a gleam of cynical amusement in his pink-bordered eyes. "No, I guess Osgood can't fix the blame on you, Miss Danziger, hard as he's trying. He's playing games the way they all do, hoping he might get lucky. But you've given me more work now. Since there's really a second key, I'll have to go hunting for it up at the main house."

"I'm sorry," Adriana said, matching his smile with a small, rueful one of her own.

Minutes later she was aboard the *Monica-Mae*, her suitcases neatly stowed under a tarpaulin beside her. As they chugged away from the jetty, she glanced back at the white-brick cottage with its terra-cotta tiled roof. Automatically her eyes were drawn to Nigel's living room window, and she suddenly realized how he had gotten rid of the second key. Yes, she thought, of course! He tied it to the balloons. He tied it to the three orange balloons, and let the wind carry it out to sea. A brief, joyless laugh broke from her lips. Henry Coombs, who was coiling a hawser nearby, looked at her covertly for a moment before returning to his task.

By the end of the week Edward Osgood had been transferred to the county jail, where he soon began to complain of headaches, nausea, and insomnia. The medicines he was given helped little. One morning he was very agitated and told a guard that there had been a big black rat in his cell during the night. The guard asked him how a rat could enter a concrete building with steel doors. Osgood said he didn't know, but that it had been there all the same. From then on he spoke of the black rat to anyone who would listen to him, usually in a wild and fearful manner.

After their fifth consultation, the lawyer assigned to his case advised him to plead diminished responsibility, which would give him some chance of avoiding a mandatory life sentence, though it would mean being sent to an institution for the criminally insane.

The very next morning a guard found Osgood dead. He had ripped the sleeves from his shirt, made a noose of them, fixed it to the grating on his window, and hanged himself.

On the afternoon of the same day, Nigel Vaughan escaped from Parkstone Hospital. Dressed in a doctor's white smock that he had snatched from a passing laundry cart, and disguised by a small moustache that he had fashioned out of two flesh-colored Band-Aids and a tuft of horsehair plucked from a leather settee in the head nurse's office, the lunatic brazenly strode past the front desk and through the main gate into the parking lot. There, he managed to beg a ride into town from a congenial elderly black gentleman, who had been to the hospital to see his schizophrenic sister.

A month later, when Adriana made her promised visit, Nigel was still at large.